## She coul

Maddie's heart was pounding hard...too hard. What was wrong with her? This was Quinn Murphy, the guy who'd rejected her years ago. The guy who'd humiliated her publicly.

But when he touched one finger to the inside of her wrist, she trembled.

"I don't mix business with pleasure," he said.

"Me, either," she managed to say.

"I don't sleep with the boss."

"I don't sleep with employees."

"All good policies," he murmured, bringing her hand up to his lips and kissing her palm, "but I'd make an exception for you."

She tried to slip her hand out of his, but he pulled her closer.

"How about it, Maddie?" he said, pressing his mouth to the pulse in her wrist. "You interested in a swim?"

"I...didn't bring a swimsuit."

He brushed the tips of her fingers against his lips and whispered, "No problem."

Dear Reader,

We all have parts of our lives we'd rather not revisit. Maybe it's high school, where we felt awkward and geeky and completely uncool. Maybe it's a job or a boss we hated. Or maybe a time when we failed at something. Whatever it is, it sits in our mind with a huge sign that reads Do Not Enter—Bad Memories Ahead.

What if you had to go back to the place or the people you'd vowed to avoid for the rest of your life? What if you'd made a fool of yourself over a man, and now you had to do business with him? How would you handle it?

It's always fun to write about an ugly duckling who turns into a swan, and I loved sending Maddie back to the town where she felt like the ugliest of all the ducklings. I hope you enjoy her journey as she reconciles with the town of Otter Tail, falls in love with Quinn and discovers that, sometimes, the place we least want to be can become the place that we least want to leave— the place that feels the most like home.

Enjoy this first of four books about Otter Tail and the people who call it home!

I love to hear from readers. Visit my Web site at www.margaretwatson.com or e-mail me at margaret@margaretwatson.com.

*Margaret Watson*

# An Unlikely Setup
### Margaret Watson

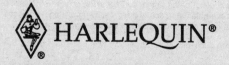

HARLEQUIN®

TORONTO • NEW YORK • LONDON
AMSTERDAM • PARIS • SYDNEY • HAMBURG
STOCKHOLM • ATHENS • TOKYO • MILAN • MADRID
PRAGUE • WARSAW • BUDAPEST • AUCKLAND

Recycling programs
for this product may
not exist in your area.

ISBN-13: 978-0-373-71608-1

AN UNLIKELY SETUP

Copyright © 2010 by Margaret Watson.

This is a work of fiction. Names, characters, places and incidents are either the product of the author's imagination or are used fictitiously, and any resemblance to actual persons, living or dead, business establishments, events or locales is entirely coincidental.

This edition published by arrangement with Harlequin Books S.A.

® and TM are trademarks of the publisher. Trademarks indicated with ® are registered in the United States Patent and Trademark Office, the Canadian Trade Marks Office and in other countries.

www.eHarlequin.com

Printed in U.S.A.

## ABOUT THE AUTHOR

Margaret Watson has always made up stories in her head. When she started actually writing them down, she realized she'd found exactly what she wanted to do with the rest of her life. Almost twenty years after staring at that first blank page, she's an award-winning, two-time RITA® Award finalist who has written more than twenty books for Silhouette and Harlequin Books.

When she's not writing or spending time with her family, she practices veterinary medicine. She loves everything about her job, other than the "Hey, Dr. Watson, where's Sherlock?" jokes, which she's heard way too many times. She loves pets, but writing is her passion. And that's just elementary, my dear readers. Margaret lives near Chicago with her husband and three daughters and a menagerie of pets.

### Books by Margaret Watson

**HARLEQUIN SUPERROMANCE**

For all my friends who make Quigley's nights so
much fun, but especially Pat and Jack Herr,
Marcy and Steve Anderson, Helen and
Stephen Baggett, Nancy Quigley and Jeff Root.

And thanks to PBJ for providing
the soundtrack to our fun.

With appreciation to Chelsea Schafer
for her expertise and invaluable help.

# CHAPTER ONE

FATE SURE HAD A WAY of biting you in the butt.

Of all the places she could have gone to lick her wounds and regroup, why did it have to be Otter Tail, Wisconsin? The town was the symbol of everything she'd once hated about her life. As a young teen, she'd been sent to spend the summers here with her godfather, David. In spite of her love for him, she'd felt isolated and alone. Too shy to make friends with the local teens, she'd felt like a failure. A freak. An outsider. When she was sixteen, she'd vowed never to return.

Yet here she was, fifteen years later, the weight of failure again heavy on her shoulders, steeling herself to drive into this depressing excuse for a town.

Fate was no doubt laughing her ass off right now.

Maddie Johnson put on her sunglasses, tightened her grip on the steering wheel and accelerated her small SUV around the final curve. Moments later, at the bridge, she screeched to a halt.

When she'd last seen the town, it had been a tired place, its fortunes sagging as much as the porches on its old Victorians. Now those Victorians on Main Street were all repaired and freshly painted in rainbow colors.

Bright blue, green and yellow banners fluttered from the lightposts in the downtown area, touting Door County's newest vacation paradise. Large white boats, fishing rods sticking up like bristles on a brush, bobbed in the Otter River.

Even the old pier had been refurbished. The rusting sheet metal that used to line the concrete walls guiding the river into Lake Michigan had been replaced with a mural of leaping fish and happy fishermen. The paint glowed in the setting sun.

There was no other traffic, so Maddie paused, staring at the sight. What had happened in Otter Tail?

She put the car back in gear and crept across the bridge, looking for the first of the two pieces of property she now owned. At least the old bar wouldn't have changed. David hadn't had the time or the energy to renovate The Office.

But when she reached the building at the edge of town, she barely recognized it. It wasn't called The Office anymore. And it was far from run-down and shabby.

The hand-painted sign that hung over the door said The Harp And Halo, an Irish Pub.

It looked like…a pub in Ireland. The windows were leaded glass. The peeling, faded wooden siding had been replaced with dark, sturdy boards. The door was wood and glass, and the building looked warm and welcoming.

And busy. The parking lot was almost full, and there were more cars parked on the street. She could see a crowd through the front window.

What had happened to The Office? And why hadn't David told her about it?

Maddie parked in the last space in the lot and walked in. The bar was a long sweep of dark green marble and polished oak. Guinness posters and pictures of green fields and misty mountains hung on the oak-paneled walls. It was hard to see the decor through the people filling the tables and standing two deep at the bar. And there were just as many women here as men—that wouldn't have happened at the old Office. That dark, dreary place had been strictly male territory.

The bartender straightened and Maddie figured out one reason there were so many women in the pub. He was tall, broad-shouldered and solid, and his wavy black hair was just a little too long. His black polo shirt, stretched across a taut, muscular chest, showed off his ropy biceps. When he glanced her way, she saw his eyes were bright blue.

Maddie froze. She knew those eyes.

"What can I get you?" he asked, his voice low and intimate despite the crowded room.

Caught. Now she'd have to spend a few of her closely hoarded dollars for the privilege of checking out the business she owned.

And the man who worked behind the bar. "Guinness," she answered, annoyed to find her voice breathless.

His gaze narrowed and he studied her for a moment too long. Then he nodded. "Coming right up."

A few minutes later he set a perfectly built glass of the dark stout in front of her, a shamrock drawn in the foam. "You want to run a tab?"

Who would have thought Quinn Murphy capable

of such whimsy as shamrocks in Guinness? "I won't be here that long," she said, uneasy being the focus of his attention. Quinn wouldn't remember her, she assured herself.

Would he?

"Five bucks," he said.

She counted out six singles and slid them across the bar as she eyed him covertly. Mad Dog Murphy. That's who eighteen-year-old Quinn had been. With no mother at home and a father who drank, he'd run wild, revving his motorcycle as he roared down Main Street, raising havoc in the sleepy fishing town.

Shy, pudgy Maddie, known as Linnie back then, had secretly yearned to ride on the back of that motorcycle of his. He'd been a couple of years older and, other than that one disastrous night, he'd never noticed the awkward kid she'd been. But even at sixteen, the sound of his motorcycle rumbling down the street had made her quiver in all the right places.

Every other girl in Otter Tail had noticed Quinn, too.

And he'd noticed them right back.

Maddie leaned against the wall as Quinn worked the bar. He was in constant motion, pouring drinks and chatting with his customers, never lingering too long with any one of them. When he turned toward her end, nerves twisted in her stomach. *Would* he remember her?

One woman leaned farther over the bar than necessary when she gave Quinn her order, allowing a prime view of her cleavage. He ignored it.

Lots of things had apparently changed in Otter Tail.

Maybe he was married. Or involved.

The thought of a domesticated Quinn made Maddie take a quick drink of her beer. What kind of woman could tame him?

Stupid thought. She wasn't here to do any taming. Of Quinn or anyone else.

Quinn reached for a rag and wiped down the marble surface. An older man with bushy gray hair, wearing suspenders over his less-than-flat belly, pushed a glass toward him, signaling for a refill. When he took the glass, the man said, "A condo developer contacted me today, Quinn. He was looking for property here."

"Is that so?" Quinn yanked the beer tapper forward.

"He's not interested in the land the Harp is on," the older man assured him. "It's not close enough to the water."

"Good thing, isn't it, Gordon?" Quinn answered. "Because as far as I know, it's not for sale."

"You haven't heard from the new owner?" Gordon set his elbows on the bar and watched him carefully.

"Not yet."

Maddie's hand tightened on her glass. If she was smart, she'd set her beer down and walk out the door. But she wanted to hear the rest of the conversation.

"Maybe she's already sold the place." Gordon glanced around, as if assessing the pub's value. "This is a prime piece of property. Could be real commercial."

Quinn froze, then shoved the tap back in place as he set the beer on the counter. "Last time I checked, this place *was* commercial, Mayor Crawford."

"You know what I mean," the other man said impatiently. "Piece of property this size, we could get a big national retailer in here. Really put Otter Tail on the map. If the new owner is smart, she'll sell the place. She'd make a bucket of money."

"And so would you," Quinn said. "It's killing you that you can't get in touch with her, isn't it? I bet you're dying to sign her up with your real estate office."

"I just want to do what's best for the town," Gordon protested.

Another man, thin and wiry, with dark blond hair brushing his collar, turned and scowled at Gordon. "Give me a break, you old windbag. You want to make a bucket of money on a commission."

On *her* property. Maddie took another drink as Gordon shrugged, apparently not offended. "I'm trying to take care of my town, Paul," he said. "If I can earn a living at the same time, so much the better."

Quinn slid a beer to another customer. "Give it up, Gordon. No one wants to hear your campaign speech. We know all we need to."

"And we know all we need to know about you," Gordon retorted, all the joviality gone from his expression. "Temple didn't think enough of you to keep his word about selling you this place."

Quinn's knuckles whitened as he busied himself refilling the bowls of pretzels on the bar. "Careful, Gordon," he said quietly. "People might realize you're not Mr. Nice Guy. And then where would you be?"

Without waiting for an answer, he moved away, talking to customers and refilling drinks. The conversation with the mayor was clearly over.

Maddie leaned against the bar, suddenly dizzy. David had promised to sell the pub to Quinn? She'd be negotiating with him? The knot in her stomach tightened.

It didn't matter who she negotiated with. She had to sell this place, and fast. Her friend Hollis couldn't afford to lose the money she'd given Maddie, and the contractors were waiting to be paid. If she didn't give them all some money soon, there would be liens on the houses she was trying to sell.

Making them that much harder to market.

As Quinn poured drinks, Gordon stared at him for a moment, then moved away. The man they'd called Paul watched him go as he sipped his beer.

Quinn said something to one of the customers, then turned away, smiling. Maddie needed to talk to him. But this wasn't the time or place, she realized with a coward's relief. She'd wait until they could speak privately.

Before she could set her pint down and leave, a rough voice said into her ear, "Hey there, beautiful. Can I buy you a drink?"

Maddie jumped, sloshing some of her Guinness onto the floor, and turned to find a tall, beefy man standing too close. He had a blond buzz cut and his thick neck topped a body that had once been athletic but was now running to fat. She stepped back. She remembered J. D. Stroger, too.

"No, thanks," she said. "I'm fine."

"Then how about a dance?" He leaned closer and his beery breath washed over her.

"Not interested." She moved away.

"I can make you interested," he said as he followed her, slurring his words. "Pretty girl like you shouldn't be alone on a Thursday night. It's Thirsty Thursday, you know." He swayed a little as he loomed over her.

Great. Not only did she have to deal with J.D., but he was drunk. She glanced over her shoulder. "I like being alone. I don't want a beer, I don't want to dance with you, and I don't want to get to know you."

J.D.'s smile twisted into an ugly sneer. "Now that's downright unfriendly, city girl. Why don't I show you how things are done in the country?"

"Go away." Maddie tried to evade him, but he clamped a hand on her shoulder.

"I'm not done talking to you," he said. The people standing close froze to look at them.

"Too bad. I'm done talking to you." Maddie shoved his hand off her shoulder. "Don't touch me again."

The crowd went silent. A man called, "Back off, J.D. Don't give her the wrong idea about Otter Tail."

J.D.'s face got red and he grabbed her wrist. "You're gonna dance with me."

Maddie twisted her arm and jerked it upward, breaking his hold on her. She dodged out of his reach as he stumbled backward. Out of the corner of her eye, she saw Murphy hurrying toward them. Two men behind J.D. tried to grab his arms, but he shook them off as he lunged at her with a roar of anger.

She sidestepped him easily. "Now that's just plain pitiful," she said as he lurched into the wall. "Go home and sleep it off, J.D. No one likes a man who can't hold his liquor."

As she set the glass on the bar, Murphy grabbed J.D. from behind. The bartender glanced over his shoulder and said, "Rusty? Willis? Get him out of here."

Without waiting to see what happened, Maddie left. She'd almost made it to her car when she heard footsteps behind her. "Hold on," Quinn Murphy said.

She turned around slowly, trying to gather her composure. "Yes?"

"Are you all right?" he asked.

"I'm fine." Some of the tension drained out of her shoulders. "But thanks for stepping in."

"Sorry I had to." He watched as two men half carried J.D. from the bar. "You want to press charges?"

"For what?"

"He grabbed you. More than once." J.D.'s friends helped him stagger toward a pickup. "Want me to call the sheriff?" One side of Quinn's mouth turned up and Maddie's pulse jumped. "It wouldn't be the first time J.D. spent the night as a guest of the county."

"No, thanks." The two men stuffed J.D. into the passenger seat of the truck, and he sprawled on the bench seat, his eyes closed, listing toward the window. "He didn't hurt me."

"Your call," Quinn said, frowning. "You look familiar. Have we met before?"

She wasn't about to remind him. "I'm from Chicago," she said. "I doubt it."

He crossed his arms over his chest without taking his eyes off her face. "You just passing through, or are you staying in Otter Tail?"

"I'm staying here. For a while, anyway."

"On vacation?"

"A combination of business and vacation." She hesitated. This wasn't the time to do business. He had people waiting for him inside. "I'm a...writer." She would be, if she could find another newspaper job. "I'm working on a story." It was called "How to Dig Yourself Out of a Huge Hole."

"Yeah?" He gave her another of those mouthwatering grins. "What do you write? I'm a big reader."

Quinn Murphy a reader? That was unexpected—and intriguing. "Nonfiction," she said. "I'm trying to get published."

It seemed like forever since she'd been laid off from her job as an investigative reporter for the *Chicago Herald* and started buying houses to rehab. In reality, it had been less than a year. Who knew you could get into so much trouble with real estate in such a short time?

"Can I buy you another beer to make up for J.D., Ms....?" He stuck his hand out and waited expectantly.

"Maddie," she said.

"Quinn Murphy." He engulfed her hand in his much larger one. Maddie was not a small woman, but she felt dwarfed by Quinn. He was a head taller than her and solidly built. "Welcome to Otter Tail." He held on to her a heartbeat longer than necessary.

"Thank you, Mr. Murphy," she said, tugging slightly.

"Call me Quinn." He smiled as he slid his fingers away from hers. Too slowly.

Her skin tingled, and she swallowed. This wasn't the way she'd wanted to spend her first evening in town.

"Coming back in, Maddie?" he asked. "You look like you're wound a little tight. I'd hate to have you leave the Harp with a bad impression."

Wound tight. Yeah, she was that. On the drive up from Chicago, she'd felt like a spring, ready to bounce through the roof. "I don't know. One beer is my limit."

"Be reckless tonight," he said, his eyes twinkling. "Let me buy you another one."

Suddenly, ignoring her better judgment, she wanted to be reckless. She wanted to see Murphy smile again. "All right. I guess one more won't hurt." Maybe it would let her relax enough to sleep.

"Great." He touched her lower back, steering her toward the door, and her skin burned beneath the thin sweater she wore. "When things slow down, you can tell me about your book."

Smooth line. But then, Quinn had always been smooth. The boys had all wanted to be Quinn. The girls had all just wanted him. "Looks like you do a good business here," she murmured.

"I do okay," he said as he opened the door for her. The bar sounds rolled over her. "It'd be easier if I had more help."

"I saw your sign." She nodded at the Waitress Wanted in the window. "Are you that tough to work for?"

"I'm the easiest boss in the world, as long as you show up on time and do your work." His gaze sharpened. "You interested in the job?"

"Of course not. I'm not going to be here very long." She hoped.

He shrugged. "If that story gives you writer's block,

let me know. I'd hire you even if you're only going to be here a week or two."

"How do you know I'd be any good as a waitress?" Although she was. She'd waitressed her way through college. "I could be the biggest klutz in the world."

"I saw you handle J.D.," he said as he stepped behind the bar. "You're no klutz." He pulled her a glass of Guinness and set it on the counter. "Sam, get off that stool and give it to the lady," he said to a young man staring into his beer.

The kid jerked to attention. His fair complexion turned beet red and he stumbled to his feet. "Sorry, ma'am," he muttered. "I didn't see you."

"Thanks. That's very sweet of you," Maddie said with a smile.

His face became darker red. "I was going to play some darts anyway." Sam edged away from the bar.

"You scared him off," Maddie said to Quinn. "That wasn't nice."

"I'm not a nice man." Something dark swirled in the depths of his eyes, then was gone. He wiped a rag over some spilled liquid. "Besides, Sam was feeling sorry for himself, and self-pity and beer are a bad combination. He needed to get off his rear."

As Quinn filled an order farther down, Maddie eased herself onto the stool, sipped her Guinness and looked around. Quinn's pub was a popular place. Why hadn't David told her about it? Especially if he'd promised to sell it to Quinn.

She should have spent more time with David. She

should have visited him while he was sick. But he hadn't told her how serious his illness was.

She'd give Quinn the chance to buy the pub from her. She didn't care who bought the place. All she wanted was enough money to pay her creditors and return the money she'd borrowed from her friend Hollis.

Quinn was now talking to an older man in a sports coat and tie who sat at the opposite end of the bar. The muscles beneath Quinn's polo shirt bunched as he reached for a bowl of pretzels and put it in front of the guy, and Maddie found herself staring at them. Why did it have to be Quinn Murphy who managed the bar she had to sell?

Drinking the heavy, bitter beer, she forced herself to ignore Quinn. She was as bad as all the other women in here tonight, she thought with disgust. Intoxicated by the sight of a good-looking man. She wasn't desperate enough to chase after Quinn Murphy.

She caught a glimpse of Sam throwing darts half-heartedly at the board on the wall, and made an impulsive decision. Quinn and J.D. hadn't recognized her. Surely that meant her identity was safe for tonight. Sliding off the stool, she wove among the people standing at the bar, heading toward the dartboard.

# CHAPTER TWO

HE KNEW HER.

Quinn washed a glass and dried it as he watched Maddie toss another dart into the center of the board. The name didn't ring a bell, but there was something familiar about her face.

She turned to Sam, said something, and the kid laughed. The same kid who'd been crying in his beer an hour ago because he'd been dumped by Annamae Simpson.

The glass rattled as Quinn deposited it on the rack. What did Maddie find so damn fascinating about Sam Talbott?

He knew what Sam saw when he looked at Maddie—dark red hair that shot fire every time she moved her head, green eyes, generous curves and a fascinating face. She was an intriguing combination of tough and vulnerable.

And nervous.

Had been from the moment she walked in the door. Quinn made it his business to pay attention to his customers.

As he served drinks and chatted with the people sitting at the bar, he kept one eye on her, although he wasn't sure why. He normally didn't go for high-strung women.

Talbott was standing awfully close to her. Quinn shifted from one foot to the other and resisted the impulse to walk over to them. Maddie had demonstrated that she could take care of herself.

And maybe she wanted to stand close to Sam Talbott.

Quinn forced his eyes away from her. It wasn't his business if his customers got friendly. That was the point of a pub, wasn't it? To have fun and get to know people.

Why the hell would Maddie be interested in Sam Talbott? He was just a kid.

"Hey, Quinn, did the redhead over there really punch out J.D.?" Paul Black asked.

"What are you talking about?" Quinn turned to him, grateful for the distraction. "You were here. You saw what happened."

Paul snorted. "I was too busy telling Gordon what an ass he was, and I missed all the fun."

"No, she did not punch out J.D. She told him she didn't want to dance with him. That's it." Quinn shook his head. "The way gossip travels around here, I guess by tomorrow she'll have put him in the hospital."

"Probably," Paul said with a laugh.

Another man at the bar explained what had happened, and Quinn listened to them rehash the incident for about the fifth time. Everyone agreed that the city girl had made a fool of J.D. Quinn hoped she'd stay out of J.D.'s way. He turned mean as a snake when he was drunk.

Sam leaned into Maddie, nodded, then made his way to the bar. He set their glasses on the marble. "A Coke and a Bud Light, please, Quinn."

"That was the quickest recovery from a broken heart I've ever seen." Quinn shoved the glasses into the dirty dish rack.

"What are you talking about?" The kid gave him a puzzled look.

Quinn nodded toward Maddie. "You two are real cozy back there."

Sam followed his gaze. "Maddie?" Quinn had no trouble reading the lust in Sam's eyes. "She's awesome."

"Yeah, she is. Too bad she's out of your league." Quinn set the Coke on the counter and some of the soft drink slopped over the side of the glass.

"She is not." The kid's tongue was practically hanging out. Maddie was tossing darts at the board by herself, her hair gleaming beneath the lights.

Quinn felt liquid flowing over his hand, and he realized he'd opened the tapper of Bud, but was holding the glass beneath a different spigot. Swearing under his breath, he grabbed a clean glass and watched it fill.

Sam gulped his beer without taking his eyes off her. "She's really hot, for an older woman."

"Older woman?" She couldn't be more than thirty. "Don't tell her that, okay? There's been more than enough violence in this place for one night."

"Think of all the experience she's had," Sam said happily.

"You think she's going to teach you some new moves?" Quinn reined in the impulse to lean across the bar and shake some sense into him. "What's Annamae going to say about that?"

"Who cares? Annamae dumped me," Sam replied.

"She's dumped you before and you didn't come here and try to pick up tourists."

"I should have." Sam swigged back more beer. "Maddie's a lot more fun than Annamae."

Maddie laughed, drawing Quinn's attention. A couple had joined her at the dartboard.

"Gotta go," Sam said as he picked up both drinks and headed back. In a few minutes, all four of them were playing darts.

Quinn tried to ignore her for the rest of the evening, but failed miserably. Maddie and Sam now sat in a corner booth. Their heads were close together, and every time she touched Sam's hand, Quinn took a deep breath.

There were only a few people left in the pub when Quinn stepped from behind the bar to pick up the dirty glasses on the tables. Sam had taken off a while ago, and Maddie was alone, writing in a notebook.

"I guess you didn't let J.D. ruin your evening," he said.

She looked up and smiled. "I had a good time tonight. Thanks for persuading me to stay."

"My pleasure." He set the dirty glasses on a table. "You and Sam sure got cozy."

She slid to the edge of the booth and started to stand. "He's a nice kid."

Quinn steadied her by grasping her elbow, letting his fingers slide over her silky skin. "You two were having a pretty intense conversation back here."

"Sam's very sweet. He was telling me about his breakup with his girlfriend."

*Sweet.* That's not what a woman said about a man she

was interested in. Some of the tension in his shoulders eased. "He's an idiot. He and Annamae break up once a month, regular as clockwork."

Her low, husky laugh stirred his blood. "It sounded like a very tumultuous relationship."

"That's one word for it, I guess."

"What would you call it?"

"Goofballs in love. Annamae is as bad as Sam. Their romance is the fodder for endless gossip."

"Small towns are big on gossip, aren't they?" The sudden chill in her voice had nothing to do with the Lake Michigan breeze blowing in through the front door.

He tried to read her expression. "You grow up in a small town?"

"No, I grew up in Chicago. But I spent some time in small towns when I was a kid."

"Not a good experience?"

"Let's just say I never went back."

"Otter Tail is a nice place. Not everyone is like J.D.," he said. "He's not a bad guy, but he's been out of control since his wife divorced him. Stay away from him while you're here."

"Don't worry. He's not my type."

"Good to hear it." Quinn edged a little closer. "What *is* your type?"

"It's not bullying ex-jocks, that's for sure."

"How do you know he used to be a jock?"

She avoided his gaze as she fiddled with her purse. "Come on. A guy built like that, who likes to push people around? I'm guessing high school football player."

"Bingo. Give the lady a cigar." He touched her arm again and found her silky skin had cooled. "Are you going to come back to the Harp, Maddie?"

"Definitely. Although I'm not sure you'll want me here."

"Trust me. You're welcome anytime." He picked up the dirty glasses. "We aim to please. For you, we'd make an extraspecial effort."

She laughed as she headed for the restroom. "Wow, now you've made me all tingly."

He watched as she disappeared around the corner. Tingly. Yeah, that was the polite way to describe it.

After he'd washed the glasses, put them away and checked his stock, he realized Maddie had returned to the booth and was lingering over the small amount of cola in her glass. Why was she still here? Had she decided to have even more fun tonight?

Desire swept through him as he watched her, and he hurried to finish the setup for the next day. Women occasionally hung around after the pub closed, but he never took them up on their offers. Sleeping with the customers was no way to run a business.

Maybe it was time to change his policy.

Ignoring Ted Bartlett who was sweeping the floor, he walked back to the booth. "I thought you were leaving. You need something?"

She looked up, her green eyes now cautious. "I was hoping to talk to you."

He slid into the booth across from her, his hands itching to touch her again. "What can I do for you?"

"This is a little awkward," she said, swallowing.

"Don't worry, Maddie." He leaned toward her. "I don't bite. Unless you want me to."

Awareness flared in her eyes. Then she cleared her throat. "Not exactly what I had in mind," she said. "Although thanks for the offer. I wanted to tell you I'm the new owner of the pub. David left it to me."

Quinn jerked away from her. "The hell you say... You're Madeline *Johnson?*"

"I am." Her fingers whitened on her glass. "I came to Otter Tail to check on his property and figure out what to do with it."

David had promised him the opportunity to buy the business he'd built, then he'd left it to this woman, instead. Anger stirred, just as it had so many times since David died. Was Maddie David's lover? Was that why he'd given it to her?

*Don't go there. It wouldn't change anything.* He had to focus on the pub. It was all he cared about.

"Why didn't you tell me who you were right away?"

She glanced at Ted. "Did you want to discuss this in front of half the town?"

"Fair enough. Are you going to take it over? Run the place?"

"No, I'm not." Her hand relaxed on the glass. "I don't know anything about running a bar. I'm going to sell it."

That was the best news he'd heard in weeks. "Great. I want to buy it."

Something that looked like relief appeared in her eyes. "Excellent. I have an appointment with a Realtor tomorrow. I'd like to get this done quickly."

"Same goes." He let out a breath. "You're not using Gordon Crawford, are you?"

"The mayor?" Her eyes twinkled, and it felt like someone had punched him in the chest. "I heard your conversation with him earlier, and I'm happy to say no. I'm meeting Laura Taylor."

*Thank God.* "Laura will give you good advice. She's honest and straightforward. I'm willing to make you an offer right now."

A tiny crease appeared between her eyebrows. "Go ahead, but I won't commit to anything until I talk to Laura."

Ted edged closer to their table. "I think you missed a spot by the door," Quinn called to him.

Shooting him a dirty look, the older man headed away from the booth. Moving slowly.

Quinn turned back to Maddie. Her hands were clenched on her empty glass again, and it appeared as if she was holding her breath. "You want another Coke?" he asked.

"No, thanks. What are you offering for the pub and the land, Mr. Murphy?"

"Quinn." He settled into the booth. "How about $300,000?"

She exhaled in a rush. "I need a lot more than that."

"That's what it's worth. David had the property appraised after I rebuilt the pub." When he'd promised to sell it to him for that price.

"How long ago was that?"

"Two years ago." Okay, maybe he'd have to go up a little. "I can go as high as $325,000."

Maddie set the glass aside and folded her hands on

the table. "I need more, Quinn. Maybe we should wait until I talk to Laura."

"Laura will tell you the same thing. It's a fair price." He drummed his fingers on the table. "What do you think you can get for this place?"

"At least $500,000."

"That's crazy." Quinn stared at her, shocked. "That's on-the-lake, Sturgeon Falls money. Not middle-of-town, Otter Tail money. Are you sure you haven't been talking to Gordon?"

She gathered her purse. "I'll discuss your offer with Laura tomorrow," she said. "We'll get back to you."

Quinn stood up. "You do that. Maybe Laura can make you see reason."

QUINN TOOK ANOTHER GULP of scalding coffee, shifted his chair away from the sunlight pouring in through the Harp's front window, then pushed the laptop away from him. He couldn't concentrate on the spreadsheet. The only figure he could see was $500,000.

The same number that had been running in circles in his head since last night.

She couldn't get that much for the Harp.

Could she?

One of the big retailers would pay a hefty premium to get a foothold in Otter Tail.

Shutting the lid of the laptop, he stood and walked to the bar, pouring another cup of coffee. It was going to be a long day.

The front door opened and Paul Black walked in. "Hey, Quinn."

"Paul. What's up?"

The attorney eased onto a stool. "I heard the news. That the cute redhead owns this place, and she's looking to make a bundle of money."

"I bet Ted Bartlett couldn't wait to spread *that* gossip." Quinn jerked his head at the coffeepot. "Want a cup?"

"Sure." Paul waited until Quinn handed it to him. "I've been elected to talk to you."

"What do you mean?"

Paul cupped his hands around the mug. "Everyone in town's upset. They think the redhead is going to sell this place to some company that'll tear it down and put up a big box store."

"She's talking to Laura today."

"Laura?" Paul's face tightened. "She's probably on Gordon's side."

"Why would you think that?"

"She's Ms. Ambition. Ms. Straight Arrow."

"What do you have against Laura?" Quinn studied his friend.

"Forget her." Paul shifted on the bar stool and blew on the coffee. "What are you going to do about the Harp?"

"What can I do? I've made an offer. Maddie says it's too low."

"Is that all you're going to do? Say 'too bad, I can't give her the money she wants'?" Paul scowled at him. "What's wrong with you?"

"What am I supposed to do? I can't force her to take my offer."

"Quinn, I know you're big on not getting involved. You like standing off to the side." He pushed the mug back and forth, careful not to spill a drop. "But you can't just stand there this time. You have to do something. You can't let her sell it out from under you. Otter Tail needs the Harp."

Quinn needed the Harp, too. Unfortunately, Paul was saying exactly what he'd tried to ignore since last night. If he didn't want this pub, his lifeline, to disappear, he'd have to get involved. No matter how much he wanted to stand on the sidelines, he had no choice. "How exactly am I supposed to do that? I'm sure you have ideas."

"Talk to Laura. Maybe she'll stall Maddie until we can figure something out."

"What's this 'we'? Last time I looked, it was my money on the line."

"But it's the town's pub," Paul said. "The town's gathering place. And if you want to keep it, you're going to have to fight for it. We can help you."

"I'm not much of a fighter these days," Quinn said.

"Some things are worth fighting for." His friend took a last gulp of his coffee and pushed away from the bar. "Do something, Quinn."

Quinn watched Paul walk out the door into the summer sunshine. The Harp was important to him. More important than anyone knew.

Paul was right. Some things *were* worth fighting for.

He grabbed his phone and scrolled down to the number he wanted, then pushed the button. "Laura? This is Quinn. I need a favor."

# CHAPTER THREE

THE LUNCH RUSH was tapering off when Maddie opened the door to the Cherry Tree Diner the next afternoon. Laura had told her she was working out of her home while the office was painted. The bell on the door tinkled and Maddie walked into a memory.

The place had aged, but very little had changed in fifteen years. The blue vinyl of the booths had cracked and peeled, the chrome on the stools that lined the counter was duller and tarnished, and the pictures on the wall were more faded.

Other than that, it was like stepping back in time. And Laura had been right, Maddie saw with relief. There were few customers now. They'd have plenty of privacy to talk.

One of the waitresses wandered by with a pot of coffee. "Go ahead and seat yourself, hon. Menus are on the table."

The corner booth was empty, and Maddie slid in. "Coffee?" A different waitress stood next to her, also holding a coffeepot.

Another cup and her hands would be shaking, but she said, "Please," and pushed the mug at her place setting toward the woman, who promptly filled it.

"Are you ready to order?"

"I'm meeting someone. I'll wait until she gets here, if that's okay."

"No problem." Instead of leaving, the waitress studied her. "Linnie?" she said softly.

Maddie looked up sharply. The woman's dishwater-blonde hair was pulled back into a ponytail and the pink lipstick she wore was mostly chewed off. Her hazel eyes were shrewd as she studied Maddie.

"It *is* you," she said.

Maddie glanced at her name tag. Jen. She looked back at the woman's face and froze. Jen Horton. Star athlete at Otter Tail High. Blonde bombshell. And dating the most popular guy in town.

She'd been at that party fifteen years ago, too.

"Jen Horton, right? I can't believe you recognized me," Maddie said.

"Jen Summers now." She smiled. "You wait tables as long as I have, you get good with faces and names."

"I'm impressed." Especially because she looked very different than she had in high school. "Except my name isn't Linnie."

Jen raised her eyebrows. "You used an alias when you were sixteen?"

Maddie relaxed. Apparently Jen didn't remember what had happened at that party so long ago. "No," she said with a smile. "I'm Maddie, short for Madeline. My cousin called me Linnie when I was a kid, and it stuck."

"Until you transformed from an ugly duckling into a swan and changed your name to go along with it."

"I don't know about the swan part, but college

seemed like the perfect time to start over. So I began using Maddie."

"Okay, then, Maddie it is." Jen set the coffeepot on the table. "So you're the one who inherited David Temple's property."

"How did you know that?"

Jen snorted. "This is Otter Tail."

"I can't believe Quinn spread that around."

"Quinn? Mr. Closemouthed? The original island? Of course not." Jen grinned again. "Ted Bartlett cleans the pub for him. He overheard you two talking."

Maddie vaguely remembered a short, older man sweeping the floor last night. "So now everyone in town knows."

"Oh, yeah. And no one's going to be shy about telling you what they think."

"Which is…?"

"Sell it to Quinn. David promised it to him, after all." Jen frowned. "We've all wondered why he didn't do it before he died."

Maddie had no idea, but maybe she would have, if she'd visited David before he died. She felt guilty all over again. She'd been too caught up in her own problems in Chicago. "I'm meeting Laura Taylor here. I'm sure she'll be glad to take Quinn's offer under consideration."

Jen's eyes brightened. "He's already made an offer?"

"When he makes it," Maddie said. Time to change the subject. "What have you been up to since high school?"

"Don't you mean how did I end up working in this dump in Otter Tail?" Jen's smile took the bite out of the words. "I ask myself the same question every day. It's the usual story. I got pregnant when I was eighteen, so instead of going to college, I got married and had two kids by the time I was twenty. Do you remember Tony Summers?"

Maddie struggled to recall the guy.

"We ended up divorced, and I moved back here so my parents could help me with the boys. How about you?"

"I'm a reporter," Maddie said lightly, although she clenched her hands beneath the table. She wasn't about to tell Jen, Ms. Popularity, that she'd been fired.

"So you're here to settle David's estate?" Jen rested her hip against the booth, settling in.

"And visit." Since she had nowhere else to go after she'd had to sell her condo in Chicago. "Otter Tail's a nice town."

"I like it, but I never thought you did." She studied Maddie. "All the kids thought you were a stuck-up city girl. I guess we were wrong."

"Tastes change."

Jen glanced at her watch and stepped away. "My shift is over. I promised the boys we'd go into Sturgeon Falls this afternoon." She smiled, and the years fell away. Once again, Jen was the cool, gorgeous kid Maddie remembered. "See you around, Maddie-not-Linnie."

Maddie watched the other woman walk out the door. Fifteen years ago, she would never have imagined having a conversation with Jen Horton. Maybe even making friends with her.

A lot of things were different now.

Ten minutes after Jen left, another blonde around

Maddie's age walked into the diner. Her smooth bob touched her shoulders and she wore a red business suit. Not exactly what she expected in Otter Tail.

This couldn't be anyone but the Realtor.

She stood and walked toward the woman, who asked, "Maddie?"

"Yes. You must be Laura. Nice to meet you."

As they slid into the booth, they took each other's measure. Deciding how to begin.

Maddie jumped right in. "I need to sell the pub. As soon as possible."

Laura sat back on the vinyl seat. "That's blunt."

"I don't have time to play games. I need money, and I need it fast."

A tiny line appeared between Laura's eyebrows. "Mind if I ask why?"

"It's personal, and it's not important to anyone but me." She moved the napkin-wrapped silverware from one side of the table to the other. "It shouldn't affect negotiations."

"That's not true," Laura said carefully. "For instance, do you have a deadline? That could affect closing dates, and influence which offer you choose."

"You think there are going to be multiple offers?"

"I'm speaking hypothetically," she replied. "It's best to know every detail when selling property. There's a lot at stake."

"The only important thing is that I need to get as much money as possible out of the pub."

"What about the house? Are you selling that, too?"

That had been the plan, but Maddie had been swallowed by memories when she walked into the place last night. "It depends on what I can get for the pub."

"All right." Laura folded her hands and smiled at the older waitress approaching the booth. "Hi, Vonnie. Could I have a cup of tea, please?"

"I think we have a few of your bags left."

After the waitress left, Maddie asked, "This place keeps special tea bags for you?"

Laura nodded. "I give them a supply. It's easier than trying to remember to bring one with me." She waited until Vonnie returned with a pot of hot water and what looked like a homemade tea bag. "Here are some comps of recent businesses that have sold in Otter Tail. I thought you might like to look through them."

She handed over several sheets of paper, then sipped her tea while Maddie studied them. "None of these is similar to the Harp and Halo," Maddie finally said. The comps included a motel, an old hardware store in the middle of a block of buildings, and a bait-and-tackle shop near the mouth of the river. They were all listed prices far below what she needed to get for the Harp.

Laura shrugged. "Otter Tail is a small town. Our commercial properties don't turn over quickly."

"Maybe we need comps from other towns in the area," Maddie suggested.

"I can do that." She sipped her tea again. "They won't be as helpful, though. It's hard to compare prices in different places."

"What's the bottom line here, Laura? How much can I expect to get?"

The Realtor centered her mug in front of her. "That

depends on who you want to sell it to," she finally answered. "Quinn Murphy is the obvious buyer. I'm sure he's interested—David had promised to sell it to him. He'd expect to pay between $275,000 and $350,000." She shrugged. "We could probably find someone willing to pay more. Someone who'd tear the place down. There are a number of retailers who'd love to get a foothold in Door County. Many areas have strict regulations about the kind of businesses they want."

She made it sound as if selling to a big company would bring the scum of the earth into Otter Tail. Why should Maddie care who bought the property? She wouldn't be here to be affected. "How much could I get if I sold it to a chain store?"

Laura's expression was neutral, but her stiff shoulders indicated her distaste. "I'll have to research it. I haven't dealt with that kind of prospect. If we're going in that direction, the timing of the sale might be a problem, too. We're at the end of summer. A retailer would be more willing to buy in the winter, so it could build and have a store open by the following year's tourist season."

"You're telling me if I need more than Quinn's willing to offer, I'll have to wait until next spring?" Maddie clenched her hands tightly. She couldn't do that.

"We'll try, of course," Laura said delicately. "I'll be happy to list it for you, and I'll do my best to get your price. But you have to be prepared for a wait." She smiled. "I want to be up-front with you, Maddie."

"Go ahead and list it."

"Fine. I'll get a contract drawn up." She set her tea

down. "I'd suggest a preliminary inspection, too. Buyers like to know about any problems right away."

"I thought Quinn just built the pub a couple of years ago."

"He did, but things can go wrong. He did a lot of the work himself and…" She paused. "Well. We'd want to make sure he did everything right."

Why would the Realtor think Quinn had made mistakes? "How much would an inspection cost?"

"It's around $400. Then, of course, you'd have to either fix what was wrong, or disclose it to any potential buyers."

"I suppose it's a good idea," Maddie said reluctantly.

"Shall I have Quinn set up an appointment with an inspector? There's a firm in Sturgeon Falls we generally use."

"Fine. Let me know when it's going to be done. I'd like to be there."

"I will, Maddie. I want us to be on the same page, every step of the way." Laura picked up the check and slid out of the booth. "I'll be in touch."

Maddie watched her go, grimacing as she took a sip of her now-cold coffee. The Realtor had been professional, friendly and helpful. She'd been willing to look for a buyer who would pay top dollar for the pub, even though she clearly preferred to have Quinn buy the place.

So why did Maddie have a bad feeling about this?

## CHAPTER FOUR

"WHAT DID YOU DO, Quinn?" Laura asked. The Realtor strolled through the pub, touching the tiny holes in the wall around the dartboard, rocking one of the tables to make sure it was solid, and brushing the torn seat of a stool.

"What do you mean?" He poured hot water into a stainless steel tea pot and set it on the bar, along with one of Laura's tea bags, then watched as she scribbled in a small notebook. "You think I made those tables wobble and tore the vinyl there? Hell, they've been that way for a long time. But I'd gladly rip a few cushions and kick a couple of table legs if it would lower the price."

"I'm not talking about the furnishings. Those are backups, in case the inspector doesn't find anything else. Did you mess with something big?" Her gaze swept the empty room. The afternoon sunlight highlighted the scratches in the hardwood floor. He hoped she put that in her notebook, too.

"You asked me to delay Maddie. I assumed it was so you could get your financing in order. After I told her to get an inspection, I figured you'd try to put her off for a while. So why is Steve coming three days after I talked to you? Is it because you know he'll find a problem?" She crossed her arms and narrowed her eyes. "I'm fine with stalling her so you can get a bid together. But I'm not going to be part of a scam."

"Are you nuts? Anything I break, I have to fix after I buy the Harp." A good offense was the best defense. "And besides, she doesn't want the building. It's the land she's after. So who cares what the inspector finds?"

"We might find a buyer who intends to run the pub," the Realtor said.

"Not for the price she wants," he said, running his hand over the green marble. Flecks of quartz gleamed in the sun. "No one's going to pay that for a bar in Otter Tail."

"You never know," Laura answered. "She thinks she can get her price."

"I believe in the Easter Bunny and the Tooth Fairy, too."

The Realtor sighed and sank onto one of the bar stools. "I tried to talk her into taking your offer. But she insisted she needed more money," she said as she put her tea bag in the hot water.

"Did she say why?"

"No. And even if she did, I couldn't tell you."

"I should have told her to go to Gordon," Quinn said, watching Laura pour barely steeped tea into her mug. "He wouldn't have been so ethical."

"Do you have a plan?" Laura asked.

"I'm going to make sure she gets to know the Harp."

She nodded. "Show her what we'll lose."

"I'm not real sure she's going to care," Quinn said.

Maddie walked past the window, and Laura patted his arm. "Cheer up, Quinn. You might be able to come up with the money."

"Not that kind of money," he muttered as the front door opened and Maddie walked in. "Come to watch the inspection?" he said to her.

"I wouldn't miss it," she said, taking off her sunglasses and tucking one stem into the neck of her T-shirt. The shirt said Practice Safe Lunch—Use A Condiment.

He started to laugh, then caught himself. He had to fight his weakness for smart-asses. Mixing business with pleasure would be disastrous. "It's not going to be very exciting. Kind of like watching paint dry."

"Maybe," she said. "But it's my paint. So I'm going to make sure the painting is done right." She turned to the Realtor. "Hi, Laura. I'm glad you could make it."

"Of course I'm here. This is part of my job."

Maddie slid onto a bar stool and planted her elbows on the bar. It made her T-shirt tighten across her chest, and he caught an impression of lace beneath the white cotton. He forced his gaze to her face. "Would you like some coffee?"

"Thank you." When she pushed her hair away from her face, her hand trembled. "Although I've had too much already today."

"You sure you want some?" He paused with the coffeepot poised over a mug. "I have a strict rule against overserving my customers."

Her low, throaty laugh made *his* hand tremble. "Go ahead and hit me. I can hold my coffee. I won't get revved up and disorderly."

"That's a shame." He set the mug in front of her. "Might be fun to watch."

She took a drink, her hair falling forward so he couldn't see her expression. "Trust me. It's not."

There was an awkward silence in the pub, then Laura pushed a piece of paper toward Maddie. "I've begun making a list of some of the things you might want to have fixed before we put the property up for sale. Small cosmetic changes can make a big difference when you're trying to sell. Especially in this market."

"How small?" Maddie asked.

Laura nodded at the torn bar stool. "You might want to get that fixed, for instance. It's one of the first things someone's going to see when they walk in. Some of the cushions in the booths are a little lumpy. The floor is scratched. That kind of thing."

"It's a bar. Of course the floor is scratched. Of course one or two booths are beaten up," Maddie said.

"I'm just saying." Laura glanced at Quinn out of the corner of her eye as if to say *I'm trying*. "You'd be surprised how much difference a few spruce-ups can make."

"I'll keep it in mind." Maddie's hand tightened on her mug. "I'll see what the inspector has to say."

AN HOUR LATER, Maddie stared at the young man, appalled. "How can there be asbestos in the basement? Quinn remodeled the place just a couple of years ago."

"He probably didn't replace the insulation down there," the inspector said briskly.

Maddie glanced at Quinn, who shook his head.

"But there's a hole in the drywall that let me check

it," the man continued, "and I'm pretty sure that particular brand was made with asbestos. I'll look into it when I get back to the office."

"Why is there a hole in the drywall, anyway?" She looked at Quinn again, suspiciously.

He shrugged. "One of the beer vendors dropped a keg and it broke through the drywall. Those kegs are heavy suckers. I haven't had a chance to fix it."

He held her gaze as if he were as innocent as a newborn. Exposing asbestos insulation would be a great way to delay the sale of the pub, she thought.

"How soon will you know if it's asbestos?" she asked the inspector.

"It'll take a few days. Maybe as long as a week. I have to send it to a lab."

"And if it is?" she asked.

"You could just replace the drywall and leave it alone. Undisturbed, it's not a problem. But you'd have to disclose it before you sold the place."

"What if the new owners didn't want the building? What if they had another use for the land?"

"Then you've got a problem. The asbestos would have to be removed if they tore the building down. And with all the EPA regulations? It's quite a project."

"Thanks, Steve," Maddie said. She took the invoice and opened her checkbook, her hand tightening on her pen. The $375 would make her bank balance dangerously low.

After handing him the check, she watched the door close behind him. A long moment later, Quinn said, "I guess I should have fixed the wall downstairs. I'll get on that right away."

"It doesn't make any difference now." Maddie swiveled in her seat to face him. "Why didn't you fix it when it happened?"

"I figured it was a job for the new owner," he said coolly. "If I'd known how to contact you, I would have asked how you wanted me to proceed."

"You must have known it would be a problem when you scheduled this inspection," she began, then drew a deep breath when she heard her voice rising. "Yes, please fix it," she finally said. "Send me a bill."

"Will do," he said, leaning against the bar. "But I don't come cheap."

"Then I'll do it myself."

One corner of Quinn's mouth curled up. "*I'll* pay to see that."

She straightened on the bar stool. "Is that some kind of sexist crack about a woman's ability to fix things?"

"Not at all," he said, smiling now. "I'm just guessing that a city girl wouldn't have a lot of experience hanging drywall. But go ahead and prove me wrong."

She'd hung drywall, and she could repair a hole in a wall. For a moment she was tempted to tell him she'd fix it, just to wipe that smirk off his face. But sanity returned before she could, once again, leap in without looking. "I have other things I need to concentrate on."

"Quinn will charge you a fair price." Laura fixed her gaze on him. "Right, Quinn?"

"Absolutely. Might take a while, though."

Maddie slid off the stool, thinking about Hollis, back in Chicago, waiting for her money. The asbestos was a disaster, and Maddie was in no mood to spar with Quinn. "Let me know how much I owe you."

SWEAT TRICKLED DOWN Maddie's face as she struggled up a hill on County U. Ignoring her straining thighs, ignoring the heat of the sun on her back, she sucked in a deep breath and pushed to keep going. Tiny pieces of asphalt crunched beneath her running shoes and her ponytail slapped the side of her face as she ran, but she made it to the top without slowing.

Hills were good, she told herself. After the disastrous inspection that morning, she needed to run. Needed to sweat and feel her muscles work. Something to block the debacle from her mind. She needed a challenge.

That was why she ran, wasn't it? For the challenge. The workout.

Yeah, she *loved* hills.

Using the T-shirt tied around her waist, she wiped the sweat off her face. A black pickup approached, and she moved to the gravel on the shoulder of the road. But instead of passing her, the truck slowed as it got closer.

"What are you doing all the way out here?" Quinn Murphy asked.

"I'm having a tea party," she said as she veered to run around his truck. "What does it look like I'm doing?"

He raised his eyebrows. "Having a little trouble with the hills, are you?"

"I'm having a little trouble with trucks blocking my way." She kicked up her speed as she left Quinn and his vehicle behind. The engine revved as the pickup began to move, and she felt a pang of regret. Wrong place, wrong time and definitely the wrong guy.

Instead of fading into the distance, however, the truck rumbled closer. Quinn had turned around and was creeping toward her. As he pulled even, he said, "It's hot for June. Want a bottle of water?" His gaze traveled over her sports bra and running shorts. "Unless you've got one hidden somewhere?"

She untied her T-shirt and yanked it on. She'd taken it off because very few cars drove along this back road and it was so hot, but with Quinn watching her, she was too conscious of her skimpy attire.

"Hey, don't cover up for me," he protested. "I don't mind if you go shirtless. I run like that all the time."

"I'll just bet you do," she muttered, tugging on the hem of the T-shirt.

"Spoilsport." He grinned, holding a bottle of water out the window, and she slowed to a walk, then stopped.

"Thanks." She unscrewed the cap and gulped greedily. She hadn't realized she was so thirsty.

"You ran a long way if you started in Otter Tail."

She lifted her shirt to wipe the sweat off her face, and his gaze shot to her bare abdomen. She hastily dropped the hem. "I do my best thinking when I run," she said. "And there's a lot to think about today."

"Yeah? Like what?"

*Asbestos. Drywall. And a bank account that was dangerously thin.* "World peace," she said. "It's so tough to come up with a good plan."

"You've got a smart mouth." He propped his arm on

the open window as if he had all day to talk to her. "I like that in a woman."

"And I should care about your taste in women, why?"

He smiled. "Definitely a smart-ass. I have a proposition for you."

A tiny burst of heat flared in her belly. "Not interested."

"You don't even know what it is." His eyes grew heavy-lidded as he stared at her mouth. "You thought I meant...? That could be arranged, too. But I was talking business."

"What kind of business?" Annoyed with herself, she kicked at a piece of gravel on the road.

"You could work at the pub. To pay for the repairs to the drywall."

And spend that much time around Quinn? Not a chance. "I don't think so. I have too much to do."

"Like what?"

"None of your business." She didn't have anything she needed to do, really, except come up with the money to pay her bills. And this was certainly one way. But the idea of spending that much time with Quinn was unsettling.

The twinkle in his eye told her he knew it. "It could work for both of us. My last waitress quit. Said she didn't like the career path she was on. You don't intimidate easily. I like that in a waitress."

"Sorry, Quinn. I'm not going to be here long enough to make it worth my while. Or yours."

"How about a bet? If I win, you work for me. If you win, I'll fix the drywall for free."

"What kind of bet?" she asked warily. A smart woman would decline his offer and finish her run. But Maddie had never been particularly smart when it came to men. And it seemed she hadn't gotten over the crush she'd had on Quinn when she was sixteen. Or her feet would be moving.

He got out of the truck, and she couldn't help noticing how his T-shirt did nothing to hide the muscles of his chest. "You have anything you'd like to wager on?" he asked.

As he watched her, her breasts tightened beneath her sports bra, and she crossed her arms over her chest. She sure couldn't say it was due to the temperature.

"This was your idea," she told him, irritated that her voice sounded breathless. "What did you have in mind?"

He took a step closer. "I bet I can beat you up the hill."

She glanced at the work boots he wore. "In those?"

"If you're so sure you can beat me, let's go."

"Fine." She turned abruptly and ran down the hill, the sound of his heavy boots hitting the pavement behind her.

When they reached the bottom, she lined up next to him and said, "Ready, set, go!"

Her thighs burned as she raced back up the slope. Quinn was keeping pace with her, even in the jeans and heavy boots. Frowning, she pushed harder, and pulled a little ahead of him. As they neared the crest, he moved even with her.

Suddenly, he pulled off his T-shirt. His muscles rippled as he pumped his arms. Dark hair covered his chest and arrowed south beneath his waistband.

As she drank in the sight, she stumbled on a rock, and he shot past her to win.

"You cheated!" she yelled.

He smiled. "I did not. I told you I ran with my shirt off."

"That was so dirty," she said.

"Hey, it's not my fault if you can't keep your mind in the game."

"My mind had nothing to do with it. I stepped on a rock."

"Don't be ashamed that you like the way I look without a shirt." He tugged at the neckband of her T-shirt, and for an insane moment she wanted to move closer. "I like the way you look without a shirt, too."

She batted his hand away. "You think the sight of your naked body distracted me? In your dreams, Murphy."

"You should head home, Maddie." He nodded at her chest, where her erect nipples were obvious. "Apparently you're getting chilled, and I wouldn't want you to catch a cold."

She crossed her arms over her chest again, and he grinned. "See you tonight at five."

## CHAPTER FIVE

QUINN KNEW THE MOMENT Maddie walked into the pub that evening, even though his back was turned.

It was the murmur of voices, he told himself. The stirring of interest from the people already seated at the bar. That was all. He wasn't soft-headed enough to think he could feel her presence in the room. He didn't believe in that romantic crap.

When he turned, she had stopped in the doorway, uncertain. As if she wasn't sure she belonged.

The thought brought him up short. Of course she belonged. He shifted a rack of glasses and they clinked together. It was her pub, wasn't it? "Hey, Maddie," he said. "Glad you could make it."

"I said I would," she answered as she moved toward him. "I don't weasel out of my bets."

"Even though I kind of cheated?"

She smiled, and his heart hammered in his chest. "There's no 'kind of' about it. You *did* cheat. But there isn't much to do in town at night, is there? So here I am."

"There's plenty to do in Otter Tail at night." A picture filled his head—of his bed, with rumpled sheets and

Maddie's hair spread across his pillow like flames. *Not going there.* "But most of it goes on at the Harp. So you're in the right place."

"Good to know," she said too brightly. Her pupils darkened as she stared at him, as if she could read his mind. Then she ran her hands down her thighs. "Anyway, I'm ready to go."

Damn it. He forced himself to think of her as the new waitress. Nothing else.

"I honor my bets, too," he said. "I fixed the hole in the basement wall."

"Thank you." Her relief seemed out of proportion to the small task.

He nodded at her jeans and green T-shirt. "That's not regulation for the Harp. My waitresses usually wear something Irish. Plaid skirts, for instance."

"The T-shirt is as Irish as I get. So the *customers* can take it or leave it. If you expect me to wear some skanky outfit that flashes a lot of skin, I'm out of here."

His mind conjured up the way she'd looked earlier, wearing running shorts and a sports bra. "Hell, no," he said in a low voice. "If you show any skin, I'll make sure we're someplace private."

She rolled her eyes. "Oh, please."

He raised one eyebrow. "Wanna make another bet?"

"Forget it. I learned my lesson about you and bets."

"Too bad. That one might be fun."

"Stupid is more like it. That 'boss and employee' thing is always a bad idea."

Her words were as effective as a bucket of ice water. "You're right. Thanks for the reminder."

Her eyes widened. "I was thinking of you as the boss and me as the employee."

"But we both know that's not the case, don't we?"

"You're running the place. I just happen to own it."

For about the hundredth time, he wondered what had been on David's mind. Why had he broken his promise? Had it been his illness? Had he simply forgotten? Or had their friendship meant that little to him?

It wouldn't do any good to get angry. It wouldn't change anything. "My offer is still on the table. If you accept it, I'll both own it and run it."

"This isn't the place to negotiate." She glanced at the two men sitting at the bar, both watching avidly.

"You're right." He nodded at his friends. "These guys can be your practice customers. Paul Black and Patrick O'Connor."

Patrick was an older man with thick white hair, wearing a sports coat. She vaguely remembered seeing him that first night in the pub.

"Nice to meet you. Great T-shirt," she added to Paul. "But you don't say which bastards you want voted out of office."

"It's a blanket statement. Applies to whoever's in power."

Maddie laughed, and Quinn saw her relax. "Interesting philosophy."

Patrick leaned around Paul to nod at her. "Paul is our radical. He has some pretty wacky ideas."

"I'd like to hear them sometime."

"Don't say that," Quinn warned, before Paul could answer. "He'll talk your ear off."

"I'll watch myself, then. A waitress needs her ears. What can I get you guys?"

After Patrick ordered a whiskey and water on the rocks, he said, "You must be the gal who took on J.D. the other night. I heard a gorgeous redhead set him straight."

"Only in an Irish pub could you get away with that kind of blarney," Maddie said with a smile. "And I did not 'take on' J.D. We talked. That's all."

Paul snorted. "There's no such thing as a conversation with J. D. Stroger after he's had a few beers."

"Maybe not a conversation." Maddie grinned. "Let's just say words were exchanged."

Patrick smiled. "I like a beautiful woman with an attitude."

She was smooth, Quinn admitted. And she seemed comfortable enough talking to Paul and Patrick. "Come down to the end of the bar," he told Maddie. "I'll show you what to do with the drink orders after we get busy."

Before he could move, he heard a loud bang from the kitchen, then Andre began yelling. "Damn it." Quinn closed his eyes for a moment. What was the cook up to now? "Paul, will you show her the order board?"

"Glad to," his friend said.

This wasn't starting out well. Quinn wanted Maddie to enjoy the Harp. To feel comfortable here. It was his chance to make her see what she'd be destroying if she sold the Harp to someone who'd tear it down. And Andre was gearing up to have one of his nights.

MADDIE WATCHED QUINN push through a swinging door. "What's going on?" she asked Paul.

"Andre, the cook, is having another crisis," he said.

"Does he have them often?"

"Regular as clockwork," Paul assured her.

"Really? Why does Quinn put up with it?"

"Quinn says he can't find a better cook. I guess it's easier to put up with his hissy fits."

"I hope Andre is okay tonight."

"Yeah. Me, too." Paul took a drink of his black-and-tan. "My band is playing, and I hate it when there's a fight. It's distracting."

"You have a band? And it's playing at the Harp?"

"Quinn didn't tell you?"

"We didn't discuss details when I agreed to work here."

"Yeah?" Paul studied her. "What did you discuss?"

"What time I needed to show up." Changing the subject, she said, "I'll do my best to keep the patrons in line."

The door opened and Laura Taylor walked in, wearing jeans and a polo shirt. She looked a lot younger than she had wearing her red suit.

Paul scowled. "There's one patron you won't have to worry about. Laura has a stick so far up her butt she can barely sit down."

"Really? She's my Realtor, and she seems very nice."

"The woman doesn't know how to have fun."

Paul was still watching Laura, and Maddie smiled. "Maybe she just needs someone to show her how. Why don't you volunteer?"

"No way. We have different life goals, as Laura would say."

"Too bad," Maddie said. "It might have been fun for both of you."

"Not according to Laura."

TWO HOURS LATER, patrons stood shoulder to shoulder in front of the bar, and all the booths and tables were filled. Apparently, people in Otter Tail liked to go out on Friday nights. Or maybe they were here to listen to Paul's band.

Laura and Paul had carefully avoided each other. But Laura was still here.

So far, Maddie hadn't had to break up any fights. And Andre hadn't said much to her.

Paul and three other musicians were setting up at the front of the pub, and Maddie was busy taking orders and delivering drinks. She'd waitressed before, so it hadn't taken long to get into the rhythm of the Harp. And the roll of bills in the pocket of her apron was growing.

After that uncomfortable moment when he'd reminded her that she was the boss and he was the employee, Quinn had been all business. He'd been too busy pouring drinks and drawing beer to do more than keep up with her orders.

Maybe working here wouldn't be so bad.

It was an easygoing crowd, and everyone seemed to be having a good time. They were mostly locals, judging by their conversation. So many people had introduced themselves and welcomed her to Otter Tail that their names were a blur in her mind. They didn't realize she'd met some of them years earlier, when she'd been a kid. They had no idea they'd teased her about her weight and the color of her hair.

As the evening wore on, she became more and more uncomfortable. Would all these people be as friendly if they knew she was going to sell the Harp to someone who would most likely tear it down? Even though everyone called her by name, she felt like an outsider looking in.

"Hey, Maddie, you okay?" Paul Black waved a hand in front of her face.

"I'm fine," she said, pushing the guilt away. "Do you need another black-and-tan?" His beer glass was almost empty.

"No, we're getting ready to start. Could you get me a glass of cola, though?"

"Will do. Would you like something to eat before you start playing?" Quinn had told her to give the musicians food if they wanted it.

Paul shook his head. "No, thanks. I've had everything Andre makes too many times."

The menu *was* limited. The fish and chips and hamburgers looked good, and people were ordering them, but there weren't a lot of choices. People apparently came here to drink, not eat. And Andre acted as if he was doing her a favor every time he slid a plate onto the warming rack. "I'll get your soda, then."

The rest of the band stood near the front window, fiddling with speakers and amplifiers. Paul played the guitar, along with a guy with shaggy brown hair. A tall, thin man was setting up a keyboard, and a blonde woman was arranging a drum set.

As Maddie wove her way through the crowd with Paul's soda, someone tapped her on the shoulder. She glanced back at Jen Summers, the waitress from the Cherry Tree Diner. "Hi, Jen."

"Hey, Maddie. I didn't realize you worked here."

"Neither did I," Maddie answered drily.

She grinned. "Quinn can be persuasive. And it'll give you a chance to meet people."

"Everyone's been pretty friendly tonight," Maddie commented carefully. She thought she'd known everything about the place fifteen years ago. One friendly night wasn't going to change her opinion.

"That's Otter Tail. Everybody's hoping you sell the place to Quinn." Jen bumped into Patrick O'Connor and stilled. "Sorry, Mr. O'Connor," she said in a low voice.

"Jen." He nodded to her, his expression cool, and kept going toward his seat.

"Wow." Maddie watched him disappear into the crowd.

Jen sighed. "He was my math teacher senior year of high school. We had some…issues. Neither of us has forgotten, although we don't talk about it."

Patrick sat at the end of the bar. "He seems lonely," Maddie mused.

"He keeps his distance from people." Jen nudged her forward. "I was just going to say hi to Delaney. I'll introduce you."

As Maddie handed Paul his drink, Jen bent and said something to the woman with the drums, who stood and gave her a quick hug.

"Delaney," Jen said, "this is Maddie Johnson."

"Good to meet you. You're the new owner of David's house, right?" Delaney tucked her streaky blonde hair behind her ear. "David ordered a desk from me before he died, but he wasn't able to pick it up. It's still in my workshop."

"He did?" Maddie shifted her tray from one hand to the other. "Did he, uh, pay for it?"

"Paid in full." She hesitated. "If you don't want it, I can refund the money and find another buyer."

It would be nice to have the money, but David must have wanted the furniture for some reason. "Maybe I should take a look at it first."

"Great." Delaney pulled a card out of the pocket of her jeans. "Give me a call when you'd like to come over."

"Thanks."

"So you own the Harp, too," she said. "It's about time we had some new gossip in this town. Everyone's wondering what you're going to do with the place."

"I haven't decided yet." Maddie clutched the round tray to her chest.

Delaney's smile disappeared. "I didn't mean to pry," she said hastily. "Sorry."

"Don't worry about it," Maddie told her. "I'm sure everyone's wondering."

Jen was talking to Paul, so to fill the awkward silence, Maddie added, "Everyone's been telling me how good you guys are."

Delaney shrugged uncomfortably. "It's just a sideline for me. I prefer carpentry."

"You've got an interesting mix of talents. Do you build houses, too?" Maddie joked

"When I have to, to pay bills."

Maddie's jaw dropped. She'd been *kidding*.

"My true love, though, is making furniture." Delaney glanced at her drum set, then picked up the glass of iced tea Maddie had delivered earlier. "So you're taking Crystal's job. I'd heard she quit. She didn't think the work was upwardly mobile enough." She relaxed enough to smile. "You want my opinion, I think her definition of upwardly mobile was getting into Quinn's bed. When he didn't cooperate, she took off."

"He didn't tell me that."

Jen turned away from Paul. "Quinn is so used to it by now that it probably doesn't register. When he came back three years ago, every woman in Otter Tail made a move on him."

Maddie couldn't help glancing at the bar. Quinn was talking to Patrick O'Connor. She forced herself to look back at Jen and Delaney. "I thought Quinn grew up here. He hasn't lived in town his whole life?"

"He was a cop in Milwaukee for a long time," Jen said, swigging her beer. "He opened the pub two years ago."

Someone grabbed Maddie's arm. "I need another Leinie," the man bellowed. He was swaying on his feet, and his eyes were bloodshot and bleary.

"It's going to take me a while," she said in a calming voice. She urged him toward a table that had just been vacated. "Why don't you have a seat and listen to the band?"

"I don't want to listen to the band," he slurred. "I want another beer."

"Take it easy, Doug." Another man stepped between them. "Let's go play darts."

God in heaven. Maddie wove her way after them. A drunk with a dart in his hand?

Before she reached them, a couple stopped her.

"Could we get a couple of cheeseburgers with grilled onions?" the man asked.

"Sure." Maddie scribbled on her order pad. "Anything else?"

"How about a tossed salad?" the woman asked.

"No problem." She glanced at the drunk, who'd lost interest in the darts and was now heading toward the door. Thank God. "Coming right up."

"No onions!" Andre shouted at her when she gave him the order. "I do not grill onions."

"You don't? I'm sorry, but I told them they could have them." She hesitated. "Couldn't you just toss them on the grill while the hamburger is cooking?"

"No," he snapped, pointing his spatula at her.

"All right," she said after a long moment. "But please tell me you can improvise a salad. Any salad. The woman didn't specify. I realize we don't serve salads. Normally. But just this once?"

"No salads. Coleslaw."

Maddie sighed. "I'll make the woman a green salad. Where's the lettuce for the burgers?"

"No salads." He threw a hamburger patty on the grill. "And no onions."

"Fine," Maddie said. "I'll fix the onions *and* make the salad."

"Stay out of my kitchen," the cook warned.

"Or what? You'll throw onions at me?"

Andre tossed down the spatula. "That's it. I've had it. I quit."

As he was tearing off his apron, Quinn stepped

through the door. "What's going on? I heard you two yelling all the way from the bar."

"I quit," Andre bellowed. "I do not take orders from waitresses."

"She's the one getting the orders from the customers," Quinn said mildly.

"She's telling me what I have to cook." Andre glared at Maddie. "No one tells me what I cook."

"A customer asked for grilled onions on his cheeseburger and his wife wants a salad," Maddie said impatiently.

Andre shook his finger at her. "I decide what's on the menu. Not you."

"Knock it off, Andre. We've got a full house tonight. Save the drama for when it's slower. Make the damn onions and the salad."

Andre sucked in a breath. "You're taking her side over mine?"

Silence fairly reverberated through the kitchen. Then Quinn said, "Fine. You want to quit? Get out." His voice was low and deadly. "And don't come whining to me tomorrow to get your job back."

Andre's eyes widened. "You're firing me?"

"No. You quit, and I'm sick of your tantrums. You're not the only cook in Otter Tail."

"You think so?" Andre's glance at Maddie was full of venom. "Go ahead and find someone else."

He stalked to the kitchen door and pushed through it. Quinn and Maddie watched it swing shut behind him.

## CHAPTER SIX

ANGRY AT ANDRE, but more angry at himself because he'd seen this coming and ignored it, Quinn turned on Maddie. "You work here one night and you make my cook quit? What's the matter with you?"

"Maybe I shouldn't have argued with him," she said, her back stiffening. "But I didn't *make* him quit. Why don't you have a reasonable menu?"

"I should have known this would be a mistake. You think because you own the place you can say anything you want?" This was all David's fault.

"*Mistake* is exactly the right word." Her eyes flashed as she reached behind her to untie the apron. "I'll be more than happy to leave."

He clenched his teeth and struggled to get a grip on his temper. "Fine. You're right. It wasn't your fault." He adjusted the temperature on the grill with a vicious twist. "Andre was a major pain in the ass. I should have gotten rid of him a long time ago. Are you satisfied?"

What the hell was he going to do for a cook?

"You should have said something to me," she muttered. "I would have been more careful."

"Couldn't you tell he was temperamental?" Quinn grabbed a spatula and scraped the grill with hard strokes.

"Temperamental? He's a nut job." She gestured toward the stove. "What kind of chef won't cook onions?"

"Andre has his quirks, but he has me by the short hairs. I haven't been able to find anyone else."

"How hard have you looked?"

Quinn's head felt as if it were going to explode. "You're the owner. Since you think it's so easy, maybe you should find a new chef." He threw two hamburger patties on the grill. "In the meantime, go take over at the bar. Try to hold down the fort while I put this order together."

"I'll do it," she said, shouldering him aside. "I'm the one who made Andre quit. You get back to the bar."

The brief touch sent fire shooting straight to his groin, and that made him angrier. "Have you ever cooked in a restaurant?" When she didn't answer, he said, "That's what I thought. Get out of here before you destroy my kitchen."

"How tough can it be to fry a hamburger and make a couple of salads?" she asked.

He'd grabbed her by the shoulders to move her away from the grill when the swinging door to the kitchen opened and Jen walked in. "Are you okay, Maddie?" Then she saw him. "Oops. Sorry."

"Oh, for heaven's sake," Maddie said, twisting away from him. "Quinn and I were just having a discussion."

"Yeah, I've called it that, too." Jen grinned as she backed out the door.

"Wait a minute," Quinn said. Jen Summers would tell

everyone in the pub he was in the kitchen making out with the new owner, and he'd never hear the end of it. "Andre quit. We're trying to figure out who's going to cook. Would you go stand behind the bar and pull beers until we get this straightened out?"

"He quit?" Jen raised her eyebrows. "I heard the commotion. When Andre stalked out, I was afraid he'd left Maddie bleeding on the floor."

"God. Both of you get out of here!" Quinn grabbed the apron from Maddie and herded her and Jen toward the door. "I'll tell everyone the kitchen is closed."

"You don't have to do that," Jen said quickly. "I can run the kitchen for you the rest of the evening."

Quinn shook his head. "Thanks, Jen. I really appreciate that. But this isn't like cooking at home."

"I work in a restaurant," she said, grabbing the apron from him. "I want to cook at the Cherry Tree, but Benny's too territorial." She glanced at the order slip hanging above the counter. "Two cheeseburgers with grilled onions and tossed salads coming up."

"Jen, get out of my kitchen," Quinn said.

"No, let her do it," Maddie interjected.

Quinn rounded on her. "You've worked here for three hours and you're telling me how to run the business? You may own the building, but this is *my* pub. I'm still making the decisions around here."

"You just told me to find a new cook. I did. So let her."

Jen already had the apron on, and Maddie stood with her hands on her hips, daring him to contradict her.

"Fine. Get your ass out there and keep taking drink orders."

He slammed through the door. As it swung behind him, he heard Jen say, "That went well."

Still angry, he ducked beneath the door at the end of the bar. The familiar smells of spilled beer and pretzels greeted him, and he sucked in a deep breath to steady himself. The Harp was *his*. He ran it the way he wanted. Where did Maddie get off, waltzing in and ordering him around?

He could curse David. Hell, Quinn would have been happy with a long-term lease. But instead some woman no one had ever met now owned his place.

"Earth to Quinn," someone called. "How about another?"

As he built Jed the Guinness, another customer—Ian Hartshorn—asked, "What's going on with Andre?"

Damn it. Quinn slammed the tap into the off position. This would have to happen on a night when half the town was here. "He quit."

He set the glass on the bar, and Jed Burns frowned. "There's no shamrock on the foam."

"We're out of shamrocks, Jed." Quinn glared at him, and the man finally walked away.

No shamrocks tonight. His hands were shaking too badly.

"Who needs another drink?" he called. *Besides me.*

His gaze went to the half-full bottle of Jameson in one of the glass-fronted cupboards above the bar. Now dusty, it had sat untouched for two years. It would stay there today, too, he vowed. No redhead with an attitude, even the one who owned his pub, was going to make him take that bottle down.

Paul's band struck a few chords, and Quinn took a deep breath as the customers turned to watch. The music would give him a chance to calm down. No one would pay any attention to him while the band played.

Maddie worked her way through the crowd, taking drink orders, a smile plastered on her face. When she headed toward the bar, though, she dropped the smile. She didn't quite meet Quinn's eyes when she lined the slips of paper up on the end of the counter.

Not exactly the way he'd planned on making her feel welcome and part of the town and the Harp. *Don't think about her.* He had to get through the rest of the evening without losing it.

Quinn heard the first notes of a Fleetwood Mac song, and the bar went still. Everyone watched Delaney set down her drumsticks. They knew what was coming.

Her liquid voice poured out and washed over the crowd. Maddie had been delivering drinks, but when she heard Delaney, she stopped and stared.

Delaney had that effect on people the first time they heard her sing.

Time seemed to stand still until she finished the song. Then the band started an old Creedence Clearwater piece, and everything snapped back into place.

MADDIE'S FEET ACHED by the time the last customer left the Harp, but she didn't sit down. She refused to show any weakness to Quinn, who'd been glowering at her all night. "What side work needs to be done?" she asked.

He looked up from washing glasses. "Silverware has

to be rolled into napkins. Tables washed. Condiment bottles cleaned and refilled. Ted will put the chairs on the tables when he mops the floor."

"All right." She grabbed a stack of napkins and the clean utensils, and sat at a table to roll them up.

"No suggestions on how to do it better?"

"Knock it off," she said wearily. "I'm not in the mood for a fight." She was so tired she could have fallen asleep sitting up. It had been a long time since she'd waitressed. She'd forgotten how hard it was.

"Since you're pushing yourself into *my* business, how did you know David, anyway?"

The air around Quinn was heavy with the weight of his anger. Part of her understood. If David had promised him the bar, he had a right to be upset. But she hadn't forced David to leave it to her. Heck, she hadn't even known about the Harp.

"He was a friend," she said coolly. She wasn't about to tell Quinn how much David had meant to her. It would be like a deer rolling over and exposing her belly to a hungry wolf.

"A *friend?*" His gaze swept over her slowly, and her stomach churned at the hardness in his expression. "David had good taste, I'll give you that. No wonder he left you his property—he always said his favorite women were redheads. But that still doesn't give you the right to stick your nose in my pub."

The words hit her like a punch in the stomach. Every time David had talked to Maddie or her mother, her godfather had asked how his favorite redheads were doing. She should have known Quinn would assume she'd been involved with him. "You know nothing about our relationship."

"I know all I need to know."

"Be careful, Quinn," she said in a low voice as she pushed herself away from the table. "You're upset, but don't say things you'll regret later."

"I'm just getting started."

Had he been hiding this anger ever since she'd told him who she was?

She thought he'd been flirting, and that made her a fool. She felt like that teenager in Otter Tail again, out of place and unwanted. Fat and ugly.

She hated that she'd let Quinn make her feel that way.

And that gave her the strength she needed. No one got to make her feel bad about herself ever again.

"You can talk to yourself as much as you want. But I don't have to listen to you." She grabbed her purse from behind the bar, dumped her tips into it, then untied the apron and tossed it on the counter. "Goodbye, Quinn."

He watched her walk through the door and shut it carefully behind her. He had to admire her restraint—he would have slammed it so hard the glass would break.

Jen stuck her head out of the kitchen door. "What's going on out here? I heard you and—"

"Maddie just quit." He ran a hand over his face. "Damn it. Where am I going to find another waitress?"

"She quit and that's all you can say? Why did she quit?" Jen demanded.

"I told her to keep her opinions to herself."

She shook her head. "For God's sake. She was right. Am I so bad?"

He rubbed his face, his beard rasping against his fingers. "I let my temper get the best of me, okay? It was bad enough that David left this place to his girlfriend. When she started telling me what to do, I lost it."

"'David's girlfriend'? You didn't say that to her, did you?" Jen grabbed his shirt with both hands and shook him. "Please tell me you didn't."

"Of course I said that. Who do you think she is?"

"You're such an idiot." She let him go and sank onto a bar stool. "Have you been drinking again? Because you're sure acting like it."

"Of course not. Why do *you* think David left her his property? It's the only thing that makes sense."

Jen sighed. "She didn't tell you who she was."

"What do you mean?" he asked uneasily.

"Maddie is the girl who used to stay with David in the summer when we were kids. Remember? A little overweight, flaming red hair, bad complexion?"

"The kid who got teased a lot?"

"That was her."

"That girl's name wasn't Maddie," he said, searching his memory for a chubby, unhappy kid who looked nothing like Maddie.

"You're right. We called her Linnie. But her name is Madeline. Maddie. And I remember she called David Uncle David."

"Oh, God." The things he'd said. Her face had gotten so pale that her freckles stood out like ink spots. He'd hurt her, but she'd quickly camouflaged it, and kept a careful distance as she'd dumped her apron and walked out the door.

"Sounds like you have some apologizing to do, Quinn." Jen looked at him steadily. "And I hope she makes you crawl."

"I was a jerk." He hadn't acted like this since his last bender. And he'd sworn he never would again.

"Big time."

He gave a humorless laugh. "I wanted her to like the Harp. I need to convince her to sell it to me."

"Good luck with that." Jen propped her elbows on the bar. "So that's all that's between you? A business transaction?"

"What else would there be?"

"I saw the way you were looking at her earlier. And the way she looked back. Probably a lot of other people did, too. You were interested."

"In whether she was going to sell to me the Harp," he said. "That's all."

"You keep telling yourself that," Jen said as she straightened. She slung her purse over her shoulder. "Is that the way you want it? Or are you just too much of a coward to let yourself fall for any woman?"

# CHAPTER SEVEN

A HALF-MOON BRUSHED the tops of the trees as Maddie pulled to a stop in the driveway next to David's house. *Her house.* She had every right to be here, regardless of what Quinn thought.

She wasn't going to think about Quinn. Instead, as she got out of the car, she focused on the sky. In Chicago, she was lucky to see a few stars at night. Here they were tossed across the dark velvet sky like handfuls of glitter, so thick in some places that they looked like a smear of light.

The stars blurred and ran together, and she scrubbed her hands over her eyes. She was teary because the sky was so beautiful. Quinn Murphy had nothing to do with it.

She hurried into the house, double-checking the lock after she closed it behind her. David used to tell her that he never locked his doors. Otter Tail was a safe town, he'd said. No one would try to steal from him.

She was a city girl. She locked the door.

Maddie slowed as she walked past the living room and then the library. The hardwood floors were burnished to a rich glow. Old Oriental rugs graced both rooms, one predominantly deep blue, the other red.

She'd always loved David's house. It was still hard to believe it belonged to her.

Harder to believe she might have to sell it.

She turned on the kitchen lights. David had remodeled it recently, and she imagined him standing at the stove, talking to her while he cooked.

She ran her hand over the granite countertop and cherry cabinets. He'd been so excited when he'd told her what he'd done with the room. They'd talked about his choices for hours.

Her tears dripped onto the counter, and she swallowed to control herself. David was gone. She couldn't tell him how much she missed him. She couldn't tell him she was sorry she hadn't visited him.

She couldn't ask him why he'd left the pub to her instead of Quinn.

The kitchen had the heavy, airless quality of a room closed off too long. She raised the windows, then opened the door to the attached screened porch. A pine-scented breeze drifted in. It carried the repetitive, soothing sound of waves rolling up the beach.

She'd have to fix the torn porch screens, she thought idly as she spread peanut butter on crackers and sat down to count her tips. They'd let the bugs in, but right now she wanted the fresh air.

A few minutes later, she stared at the pile of bills. She'd made over a hundred bucks in tips.

She'd had to put up with Quinn and his sneering insinuations about her and David, too. But when a person needed money as much as she did, pride flew out the window.

Could she keep working with him?

Did she have a choice?

She shoved away from the table. No. She didn't have a choice. She owed her friend Hollis too much money. Not to mention the contractors and bank. So until she sold the pub, she'd be working at the Harp. It wasn't going to make a dent in what she owed, but she'd send her friend every dollar she could.

Turning off the lights, Maddie headed upstairs to the frilly, girlie bedroom she'd loved so much as a kid. The lace and ruffles were a little overwhelming now, but reminded her of David's kindness. He'd let her pick out whatever she wanted for the room. As she tossed and turned, she imagined him standing in the doorway, telling her good-night, like he used to do during those long-ago summers.

"You'll like it here if you just give it a chance," he'd said so many times. "Otter Tail is a wonderful town. Full of good people." Once, he'd winked and said, "Even Quinn Murphy."

She picked up one of the pillows and hurled it at the empty doorway. "Get out of my head, David."

THE NIGHT WAS PITCH-BLACK outside her window when she woke with a start. She lay still, heart pounding, and wondered what had bothered her.

Faint scrabbling sounds from the first floor drifted up the stairs, and she tensed. But as she groped for her cell phone on the nightstand next to the bed, she realized they weren't human footsteps. There was some kind of animal in the house.

Mice, probably. She'd have to set traps in the morning. As she padded down the stairs, she realized the noise was coming from the kitchen.

She flipped the light switch and saw a face with a black mask hovering in the window of the screened porch. She screamed, and the raccoon fell into the sunroom. As soon as it hit the floor, it turned and scrambled up the wall and out the hole in the screen, vanishing with a flick of its fluffy, ringed tail.

As she stared in horror after it, something metallic clattered on the floor behind the island in the kitchen. Was there another one in the house? Had that been what she'd heard? Why hadn't she shut the back door to the porch?

Grabbing the broom from the hall closet, she peered around the island. A large, furry shape rushed past her into the sunroom, its tail brushing her leg as it passed. She shrieked and jumped backward, tripping over the jar of peanut butter the raccoon had knocked down. The animal scurried up the wall and left through the window.

Maddie sidled farther into the kitchen and waited, holding the broom like a shield in front of her. After a moment, she exhaled. It was empty. No more intruders.

Except her.

She didn't belong here, just like the raccoons didn't belong in the house. It was foolish to think she could fit in. Foolish to think she would grow to like Otter Tail.

Foolish to think she and Quinn could be more than adversaries.

She headed up to her bedroom and threw her clothes

into her suitcase. Grabbing her laptop, she hurried down the stairs and into the car. She was going back to Chicago. Tonight. Being in Otter Tail wasn't solving any of her problems.

She didn't have to be here for Laura to sell the Harp. She'd put Otter Tail and Quinn Murphy far behind her.

Once in the car, she realized she was still wearing her pajamas. And she'd forgotten her shoes.

She was too tired to go anywhere tonight, but she wasn't going into the house, not when there might be a raccoon still roaming inside. The backseats of her SUV had been lowered to make a cargo area, and she crawled over the armrest and onto the rough carpet. Reaching beneath the front seat, she pulled out two small blankets and wadded one up as a pillow. She tossed the other one over herself, curled into a tight ball and gradually relaxed enough to fall asleep.

QUINN TURNED HIS TRUCK onto the narrow driveway that led to David's house, clenching his teeth as he drove over the ruts. Not David's house anymore. Maddie's house.

It was late. Too late for a visit, but he needed to apologize to her or he'd never get to sleep. After what he'd said to her, he suspected she'd have a hard time sleeping, too.

He'd been an ass. He'd known it before Jen told him who Maddie really was. Finding out that she was Linnie, the woman David always talked about, had given him a sick feeling in his gut that wouldn't go away.

Her yellow SUV stood on the driveway, so she hadn't run screaming out of Otter Tail. Not yet, anyway.

There were no lights on in the house, though. So she must be asleep. He would come back tomorrow, he thought with a rush of relief.

As he was turning his car around, he noticed a gleam of white in the back of her SUV. It looked like a leg.

Worried, he parked behind her, got out and peered through the window. Maddie, curled on her side, was sound asleep. A tattered-looking blanket pooled on the carpet next to her, as if she'd kicked it off. Her red gym shorts didn't hide much of her long legs, and she wore a ratty T-shirt with a faded University of Illinois logo. Her hair curled wildly around her face.

There was a rip in the shirt beneath her left arm, exposing a creamy white curve of breast. He shoved his hands into his pockets and forced his gaze to her face.

She looked different as she slept. Younger. Softer. Defenseless.

What the hell was she doing, sleeping in her car?

"Maddie." He rapped on the glass. "Maddie, wake up."

She rolled onto her back, her legs bent at the knees, and murmured something, but she didn't open her eyes. The gym shorts crept higher up her thighs. The worn cotton of the T-shirt tightened across her chest, clearly outlining the dark shadows of her nipples. "Maddie!" he said, rapping harder. "Come on. Wake up."

Her eyes opened and she looked around the car, clearly bewildered. When she saw him at the window, she flinched and let out a surprised yelp.

Fumbling with the hatch of the car, she opened it and

got her feet into flip-flops before stepping out onto the gravel. "Quinn? What's going on?"

"Why are you sleeping in the back of your car?"

"I was too tired to drive."

"So why aren't you in bed?"

"Raccoons," she said with a shudder. "In the house. What are you doing here?"

His eyes strayed to her T-shirt again. "Rescuing you from the wildlife, apparently."

She put her hands on her hips, tightening the material across her chest. "How did you know I needed rescuing?"

"Rescuing?" he repeated, blinking.

She followed his eyes, and pink tinged her cheeks. She wrapped her arms around herself in the age-old manner of women covering themselves.

He pulled off his sweater and handed it to her. "Here. You look…cold."

She murmured her thanks while she struggled into it. The sleeves hung down past her fingertips.

"Tell me about the raccoons," he said, clearing his throat.

She explained what had happened, and he struggled not to roll his eyes. Finally, when she described running out to her car and locking herself in, he shook his head. "I'm not sure that was smart. One of those guys might have had car keys in their pocket. You can't be too careful around raccoons."

"Jerk," she muttered, heading for the house. "I was tired. I wasn't thinking straight."

He grabbed her by the arm to stop her, then let go immediately. "Anyone who stands up to drunks and

J. D. Stroger isn't afraid of a raccoon. Why were you in the car, Maddie?"

"I was going home. To Chicago. You were right. I don't belong here."

"How do you know? Give the town a chance." He stared at the stubborn set of her mouth. "You're going to run because of a fight?"

"Why are you trying to stop me? I have to sell the Harp, and probably not to you. I tried to tell you how to run your business. You should want to get rid of me as soon as possible."

Time to eat crow. "You were right about Jen. She did a good job."

Her stiff back relaxed a little.

"So stay," he added. "I *want* you to stay. Meet everyone in town."

"I already know them."

"You knew a bunch of stupid kids fifteen years ago. People change, Maddie. Are you the same person you were back then?"

"I still don't belong here."

"You could, if you'd give us a chance."

The momentary yearning in her eyes was painful to see. Then it disappeared. "I belong in the city."

"Are you selling David's house, too?"

She turned to gaze at it. "I'm not sure." Her voice softened. "I need to, but I don't want to. I have wonderful memories of this place."

He had a lot of good memories from here, as well. Memories that had been displaced by anger since David died. "I'm sorry, Maddie. For what I said. I was an ass."

"You think?" Her face was impossible to read in the dim light of the moon. "David was older than my father, for God's sake."

"That doesn't matter when you love someone." He shoved his hands into his pockets. "Maybe I was a little jealous of him last night."

"Jealous?"

"For having you."

They stared at each other for a heartbeat, then she started for the porch. "He was my godfather. My father's best friend. There was nothing like that between us."

"I wish I could take back what I said. All I can do is apologize."

"Okay. Thank you." She reached for the doorknob. "Good night, Quinn."

"That's all you're going to say? *Okay?*"

She turned around. "You want the expanded version? Fine. It was a rough night, with Andre quitting and me being new and you thinking I was trying to tell you how to run the Harp. I get that. But I'm pissed off, and I'm too tired to keep up with you. Too tired to think straight."

She was still the woman who had taken his pub away from him. The woman who wouldn't sell it to him for a reasonable price. But she looked vulnerable in her ratty shirt and droopy shorts, and he didn't want to leave her alone. He'd bet money she wouldn't sleep again tonight.

He knew he wouldn't. "Let's go inside. I'll tuck you in."

She sniffed. "Like that's going to happen." But beneath her scowl, he saw loneliness.

"I'm sorry, Maddie. You should have told me who you were. David talked about you all the time."

She blinked a couple of times, as if she had something in her eye. "The subject never came up." She turned the doorknob. Jiggled it. "Damn it."

He followed her onto the porch. "What's wrong?"

"Nothing." She gave the door a tiny kick.

"Are you locked out?"

"Maybe I left the back door open."

"Let's take a look."

But the back door was locked, too. "David never locked his doors," he said.

"I'm not David."

That was for damn sure. He gazed at her long, bare legs again. "I have a spare key at home. Climb into my truck, and we'll get it."

"I'll wait here."

He nodded at her legs. "You'll be cold."

She curled her toes under. "I'll be fine."

"I'm not leaving you sitting on the porch wearing next to nothing." He sat next to her.

"Go away, Quinn," she said, tugging his sweater down over her knees.

"Come on." He took her hand and pulled her to her feet. "I'll make you a cup of coffee."

"Coffee?" She hesitated, then shrugged. "I'm easily bribed. I'd do just about anything for a fix right now."

"Is that so?" He caressed the back of her hand with his thumb as his stomach tightened. "I'll keep it in mind."

She jerked away. "Back off, Quinn."

She got into his truck, buckled her seat belt, then leaned her head back. She didn't open her eyes until he pulled into the driveway next to his cabin and stopped.

He'd rushed out that afternoon before going to the Harp. Had he left a mess? He couldn't remember.

What did he care? This wasn't a date. He wasn't trying to impress her.

"Wake up, Maddie. We're here."

Her eyes fluttered open. "We're home?"

*Home?* No. It was more than that. It was his refuge. His sanctuary. The only place he could truly relax. "My home, Maddie. Not yours."

# CHAPTER EIGHT

"HAVE A SEAT. I'll get the key and start some coffee," Quinn said as he opened the door. Thank goodness. It wasn't as bad as he'd feared.

Maddie didn't seem to notice anything, anyway. She stumbled to the couch.

As he poured water into the machine, she leaned back against the old beat-up leather and closed her eyes. By the time he'd measured coffee into the basket and flicked the switch, she was sound asleep.

He stifled the urge to wake her up. He didn't want Maddie sleeping on his couch. It was too intimate. He didn't bring women here. If he stayed with a woman, it was at her place. So he could leave.

Sighing, he swung Maddie's legs up on the couch and eased a pillow under her head, trying to ignore the firm muscles in her calves and the sweep of her dark red hair over his arm. She turned onto her side and snuggled into the pillow with a murmur. Quinn walked to his room and took his time pulling the quilt from his bed. When he returned to the living room, he laid it over her, tucking it in with hands that weren't quite steady. With a tiny sigh, she curled her fingers into his quilt and clutched it to her chest. Her mouth was slightly open, and a strand of her hair trailed over the quilt, a slash of fire on dark green.

He'd make her an extra key to hide outside, he decided as he headed back to his bed to sleep. It was too dangerous to have her in his house. It made him think about things better left unexplored.

HE'D BEEN UP FOR AN HOUR and had finished a pot of coffee by the time she stirred. She rolled onto her back and stretched, and Quinn watched the quilt slide off. His sweater tightened across her chest.

His sweater had never looked so good.

He jerked his gaze from the soft curves beneath the dark blue wool, to her face. Her eyes opened and she looked around, bewildered.

"Hey, sleepyhead."

She shot up, staring at him from across the room. "Quinn? What are you doing here?"

His eyes strayed to the sweater again. "Having coffee and catching up on my reading," he said deliberately. He was pretty sure she didn't want to hear that he was fantasizing about her breasts.

Her forehead furrowed. "Why are you in my—" She stopped, and he watched memory return to her. "I'm at *your* house."

"Bingo."

"I must have fallen asleep as soon as we got here. I'm sorry."

"Don't worry about it."

"I've kept you from sleeping, haven't I?" She threw the quilt off and stood.

"I slept just fine," he lied. He'd tossed and turned until he'd given up trying.

Pathetic to be turned on by a pair of faded gym shorts and his own baggy sweater. Clearly, he needed to get out more. He curled his hands around the coffee mug.

"You should have left me at David's and brought the key." She glanced out his window, where dawn was a faint glow on the horizon. "It's almost morning."

He nodded at the coffeepot. "Want some coffee?"

"No, thanks. You've wasted enough time with me. I'll make some when I get home."

"We'll stop by the Cherry Tree and get a cup. There's a lot to be said for instant gratification."

That stirred visions he had no business thinking about—her mouth fused to his, her body beneath him.

Their gazes locked, and suddenly the room was too hot. Too small. Her pupils dilated. Color rose in her cheeks. Apparently, she liked instant gratification, too.

She tried to step away from him, but bumped into a chair. She reached out to steady it at the same time he did. Their hands brushed, and neither of them pulled away.

When he touched one finger to the inside of her wrist, she trembled. He stilled, then said, "I don't mix business with pleasure."

"Me, neither," she managed to say.

"I don't sleep with the boss."

"I don't sleep with employees."

"Good policies." He brought her hand up to his lips and kissed her palm, inhaling her citrusy scent. Oranges blended with the wool of his sweater. If he didn't touch her, he'd go crazy. "I stay out of the Otter Tail dating pool, too."

"Makes things less complicated," she gasped.

He brushed the tips of her fingers against his lips. One taste. That's all he'd take. "I'd make an exception for you."

"Lucky me." She tried to slip her hand out of his, but he tightened his hold and tugged her closer.

Maddie's heart was pounding so hard she could barely breathe. This was Quinn Murphy. The guy who'd laughed at her when she'd asked him to kiss her years ago. The guy who'd humiliated her in front of the coolest kids in town.

"How about it, Maddie?" He pressed his mouth to the pulse in her wrist, and she shivered. "You interested in a swim?" His voice washed over her, a dark, rich temptation to sin.

"Sorry," she said, her body softening. "I didn't bring my swimsuit."

"No problem." He trailed a finger down her neck and her heart thundered in her chest. "I love skinny-dipping."

"You should come with a warning label," she muttered, but she didn't move away. Her body was begging her to move closer, to accept what he was offering, and she didn't have the willpower to resist. She scrambled to recall the memories of that horrible party, but her mind was full of the way Quinn felt right now, and wouldn't cooperate.

"I've been thinking about you since you walked into the Harp," he whispered. He slipped one hand into her hair, caressing her scalp, and heat washed over her. "Wanting to kiss you. Even after I found out you owned the place."

He bent his head and skimmed his mouth over hers, edging her a little closer. His chest brushed her nipples, which were hard and exquisitely sensitive against the thin T-shirt. She almost whimpered. His legs shifted, and he drew her into the vee of his thighs.

No one had ever called her a small woman, but his height and broad chest made her feel tiny. When he wrapped his arm around her and drew her against him, it felt as if his body fit hers perfectly.

Like he'd been made for her.

Before she could pull away, he deepened the kiss, and she lost her train of thought as his mouth played with hers.

His tongue slid over hers. His hips pushed against hers, matching the thrusts of his tongue in her mouth. Her hands moved restlessly over his back. He smiled against her mouth. "I want to touch you, too," he whispered.

He burrowed beneath the sweater, beneath the T-shirt, until he touched her back. She imagined she felt the individual ridges of his fingerprints.

He smoothed his other hand over the front of the sweater, tracing the pattern of cables in the wool. While her body was trembling, aching for him, preparing for him, he kept kissing her, kept teasing her with his tongue, until she had to hold tightly to him or fall down.

When he eased away, she turned her head to find his mouth again. "My God, Maddie," he muttered as he nibbled his way down her neck. "I've barely kissed you and I'm ready to explode." He nudged his hips against hers, and the hard, hot length of his erection burned into her.

He cupped her breast in one hand and she pressed into his palm, desperate for his touch. He nipped the tendon in her neck as his fingers caressed her, tracing smaller and smaller circles until she thought she would scream. When he finally brushed his thumb over her nipple, she couldn't hold back the tiny cry that erupted from her throat.

He groaned and shoved up the sweater, bent his head and took her into his mouth through the thin cotton of her T-shirt. As his teeth grazed over her, she cried out again. "Quinn," she panted. "Please."

"Please what?" He blew gently on the dampened T-shirt. "More? Stop?"

She shuddered as he suckled her through the shirt. "More," she choked out. "Stop."

He froze, his breath hot through the shirt. "Which is it, Maddie?"

Somehow, she stepped away from him, letting his sweater slide down again. She bit her lip when the wool pressed against her aching nipples.

"Stop," she repeated. Even to herself, she didn't sound very convincing. She cleared her throat. "This isn't smart."

"You're right." He lifted a strand of her hair and combed his fingers through it. "Terrible plan."

He smiled, triggering memories of that long-ago party and the way he'd laughed at her. Remembered humiliation made her cheeks hot, and she pushed his hand away. "I'm not sixteen anymore, Quinn. I know better now."

His eyes narrowed. "What's that supposed to mean?"

*Damn it!* She drew in a sharp breath. "It means I'm

not a kid with poor impulse control. It means I've learned that just because something feels good doesn't mean it's smart."

"Smart?" The sheen of desire in his eyes faded. "You're right. This was damn stupid."

She hadn't been thinking. She'd jumped in, impulsive and reckless. Hadn't she learned what happened when she let her impulsive side take over?

He grabbed his keys off the counter, and her irritation spiked. "You're not angry, are you? You started this," Maddie said. "Not me."

"I'm not angry. I'm annoyed at myself for losing focus. For forgetting what's important." He dumped the dregs of coffee in the sink and set his mug on the counter a little too hard. "I forgot my own rules."

She tugged on the hem of her shorts, trying to cover more of her legs. Suddenly, she felt bare. Exposed. And she didn't like the feeling. "I wasn't holding a gun to your head, pal."

"I wasn't holding one to yours. And you weren't stepping away."

"Yeah, because I was too bored to move."

He looked as if he was struggling not to laugh. "You always make those noises in the back of your throat when you're bored?"

"You bet. I drive people crazy at bad movies. You don't intimidate me, Murphy."

"Is that right?" He was smiling as he pushed away from the door. "I don't intimidate you and you didn't like kissing me."

"I didn't say that. It was pleasant enough."

*"Pleasant enough?"* He laughed and pulled her against him. His mouth moved over hers, and she couldn't help responding.

This was Quinn. The guy she had to negotiate with. The one part of her brain still functioning told her to stop. To push him away. But she closed her eyes. Desire returned in a rush.

He let her go and she stumbled backward. He was panting, and her own breath was loud in her ears.

Every inch of her yearned to feel his body pressed to hers. "I think you should take me back to my house," she managed to say. Before she did something even more stupid.

"God, yes." But he stood in front of her, his eyes closed, his chest rising and falling rapidly.

She reached for the door. "You coming?"

He opened his eyes, and her skin burned from the heat of their intensity. "I'll get my jacket."

She held his gaze, not allowing her own eyes to drift lower. "I'll wait in the truck."

"Good."

Maddie stepped outside into the sunrise. Pink and gold light shimmered over the horizon, streaking the sky with color. It felt as if it pulsed in time with her body.

She slid into the truck, then drew her feet onto the seat, pulling his sweater down to cover her legs. It was chilly in the morning this far north, even in August.

Quinn emerged from the house and joined her. He backed down the driveway a little too fast, then threw the truck into gear and headed toward town.

Stands of white cedar and birch trees flashed past the

window, followed by an orchard with small red apples hanging from the branches. He didn't slow down until they reached the first houses. The truck finally rolled to a stop in front of the Cherry Tree.

"Two creams, right?"

Pleasure blindsided her. He'd remembered how she took her coffee. "I can make coffee at home."

"Two creams?"

"Yes." She sighed.

She watched him walk into the diner, watched Martha Pleance, the owner, glance out at the truck. The woman's eyes narrowed as she saw Maddie. Then she turned and called to someone.

A few moments later, Jen Summers appeared and handed Quinn a white foam cup. Her gaze drifted over to Quinn's truck, too.

Jen grinned and said something to him. Scowling, he shoved his way out the door and got into the truck, handing her the cup of coffee.

"What did Jen say?" Maddie asked cautiously.

"She said she was glad to know you don't hold a grudge. When I told her it wasn't like that, she just laughed. She asked why you looked so tired." He turned the key with a hard twist. "Damn it."

"I'll talk to Jen."

"What are you going to tell her? That you like to drive around town at dawn in your pajamas?"

"I'm in shorts. Besides, she couldn't see those, anyway."

"Focus, Maddie." He pulled away from the curb, going too fast. "You're in my truck, wearing one of my sweaters, at six-thirty in the morning. What is she supposed to think?"

"What difference does it make? She's probably only slept for three hours since closing at the pub. She'll be in a fog." Exhaustion washed over Maddie, and she laid her head against the seat. How had Jen looked so wide-awake? "Unless you're afraid your reputation for not getting involved is going to be ruined?"

"I don't want to explain to every damn person that we're not...dating, okay?"

She was catapulted back to that party when she was a teen. She tried to sip her coffee to hide her reaction, but it scalded her tongue. "Don't worry, Quinn. If anyone asks me, I'll save you. I'll tell them the truth."

"Which is...?"

"That nothing happened." She stared at the houses flashing past the car window. "That I wouldn't have you if you were the last man on earth."

## CHAPTER NINE

QUINN WAS CHECKING his stock at the Harp, writing everything down. Busywork. Anything to keep from thinking about the way Maddie had tasted that morning. About the way he'd lost control.

It couldn't happen again. He'd felt raw and exposed, and that wasn't an option. Ever.

When the door of the Harp opened, he welcomed the distraction. "We're closed," he called, glancing over his shoulder. "We open at noon." Probably a tourist who didn't know his hours, but he wanted him to come back. So he smiled at the man standing in the door.

"Quinn Murphy?"

Quinn turned to get a better look at the guy. Tourists didn't usually carry briefcases. His face was tanned and his carefully groomed brown hair was graying at the temples. He wore a dark blue suit and a lighter blue tie that, together, were probably worth more than Quinn took home in a couple of weeks. Drying his hands, he said, "Who wants to know?"

The man walked toward him, holding out his hand. "Frank Gervano. Nice to meet you, Mr. Murphy."

Quinn shook it briefly. "How do you know I'm Murphy?"

The guy's gaze shifted to Quinn's left shoulder. "The bar is closed and you're here. I assumed you're Murphy."

Quinn's cop instincts snapped to attention. The guy was lying. "You assumed right," he said cautiously. "What can I do for you?"

"Do you have a moment to talk?" Gervano asked.

"Depends on what we're going to talk about."

"Business."

Quinn nodded slowly. "Sure. Can I get you something to drink?"

Gervano glanced at the half-empty coffeepot perched next to the bottles of liquor. "Coffee would be good."

After they sat down, Gervano pulled a business card out of a silver case and slid it across the table. "I represent YourMarket," he said. "I understand this property is for sale."

Quinn's hand tightened around his coffee mug. Had Maddie called YourMarket? Was she negotiating with them at the same time she was considering his offer? "You're talking to the wrong person. I don't own the pub."

"I know that. But you're running it, and I understand you've made an offer on the property."

"Who told you that?"

"That's confidential information. So it's true?"

Maddie wouldn't sell the Harp to a company like YourMarket. Would she? Acid dripped into Quinn's stomach. "I don't think it's any of your business, Mr. Gervano."

"We'll see," he said, smiling gently. "I understand the Harp and Halo is a popular bar here."

"It's a pub. And we do okay."

"We'd like you to withdraw your bid. YourMarket

doesn't like competition when it's negotiating for a piece of property. In return, if we're successful in obtaining it, we'd help you relocate to another property."

The guy didn't know that Quinn was no competition for the chain. According to Maddie, she couldn't afford to take his offer. But he'd see how far Gervano and YourMarket were willing to go. "Let me make sure I have this right. If I help you knock the price down, you'll build me another pub? Ma—Ms. Johnson is screwed, but I'm still in business. Is that what you're saying?"

"I wouldn't put it so crudely."

"Are you willing to put that in writing?"

Annoyance flashed in the other man's eyes, quickly concealed. "I've found that agreements like this are best handled with a handshake."

"I bet you have." Quinn crossed his arms. "Why would you help me rebuild the Harp somewhere else? Last time I checked, YourMarket was in business to make money."

The man smiled again. "We value the goodwill of our customers. We like to have a solid relationship with the people in the towns we serve. And the Harp and Halo is popular."

"That's not what I heard about your company, Gervano." Quinn was on familiar ground now. Talking to this guy was just like interrogating a suspect. "Ruthless and hard-nosed is what I've heard. What you're suggesting doesn't compute."

Gervano straightened the crease on his slacks. "We want to be an asset to the communities where we do business, and assisting displaced businesses is part of that plan."

Quinn raised his eyebrows. "Instead of going to all this trouble, why don't you just buy another piece of property? There's lots of vacant land around Otter Tail."

"Most communities in Door County have size restrictions on commercial buildings. This is the only area where one of our stores would be allowed."

"So go farther out. Land would be cheaper."

"Our customers want convenience. They want their stores close to home. And with gas prices where they are..." He shrugged. "No one wants to travel to shop."

"I'm not going to withdraw my bid, and I intend to win. So no deal, Mr. Gervano." Quinn had no idea how he was going to get enough money, but he wasn't going to stop trying.

He wasn't going to hurt Maddie to help Gervano out, either.

The salesman stood. "I didn't expect a decision today. I'll give you a chance to think it over, Mr. Murphy. If you withdraw your bid, it will make things easier for YourMarket. We appreciate it when people help us out. And we believe in showing our gratitude."

"Sorry. I like the Harp just the way it is now. And just where it is."

"Think carefully—my offer won't be on the table forever. Things can change fast in the real estate business. Properties lose their value for a number of reasons."

"What exactly are you saying, Gervano?" *Was the bastard* threatening *him?*

"Just that you should weigh your options." He

opened his briefcase, took out a pen and scribbled something on the business card he'd set on the table earlier. "My personal number. Call me anytime. We'd like to work with you."

Quinn watched him walk out the door, stuck the card in his pocket, then tightened his hand into a fist. *Properties can lose their value quickly.* Was he imagining things, or was the YourMarket representative suggesting that something would happen to the Harp if Quinn didn't withdraw his bid?

The cop sense that had stirred earlier flared back to life. Having been an officer left him cynical and suspicious. Maybe he'd misread Gervano. Maybe the guy was just trying to get a better deal for his company.

But Quinn would keep a close eye on the Harp.

"I UNDERSTAND, Hollis," Maddie said as she paced her kitchen. "I know you need the money. I'm doing the best I can. It takes more than a few days to sell property."

"Is there anyone who actually *wants* to buy a dive bar in the north woods?" Hollis's voice was too high-pitched, a sure sign she was stressed.

"It's not a dive," Maddie answered automatically. "It's a very nice place." She cleared her throat. "I'm working there, actually. As a waitress."

"Why? So you can try to sell it to a customer?"

Hollis needed her money back; Maddie got that. But her hand curled around the telephone. "You know what the real estate market is like," she said, trying to keep calm. "And I've already gotten one bid."

"Yeah? Then why don't you take it?"

"It's not enough. I could pay you, but I wouldn't have enough for the contractors working on my properties. I'd be right back where I started."

There was silence at the other end. Finally, Hollis sighed. "I'm sorry, Maddie. I know you're in a bad spot. But if I don't get that money back into my IRA next month, I'm going to have to pay a huge penalty. I can't afford that."

"I'll get you the money, Hollis. Okay? I promise."

"I feel like a real bitch, hounding you when you're so strapped," Hollis said quietly.

"Don't. I got myself into this mess, and you were incredibly generous to help me out. It's going to be okay." Maddie forced herself to sound cheerful. "We'll laugh about this next year." She hoped.

"Thanks, Maddie. Keep me posted, okay?"

"You know I will." Maddie closed her eyes as she hung up. Why had she let Hollis lend her money from her IRA?

Because she'd been stupid. And cocky. Sure that she'd succeed in the real estate market. Certain that her problems were only temporary, and easily solved.

She deserved to lose her shirt. But Hollis didn't.

Maddie dug the heels of her hands into her eyes. It felt as if someone had thrown sand in her face.

Only a few hours of sleep the night before would do that to you. Not to mention being responsible for the financial ruin of your best friend.

Tossing her pen down on David's beautiful cherry table, she paced through the kitchen. What if no one else wanted to buy the Harp except Quinn? What would she do?

She'd have to sell this house, as well. Sell all her memories of David and the summers she'd spent with him. She'd hated Otter Tail, but she'd loved David. She'd loved talking to him, helping him work on the house, listening to his stories about her father, who'd died when she was two.

Her mother hadn't really wanted a child. The knowledge that there was one person who loved her without reservations, one place where someone liked having her around, had been her security blanket growing up. She didn't want to sell this house.

She'd thought she could. Until she'd actually walked in the front door.

She'd do just about anything not to sell, but right now she was too tired to think straight. Even all the coffee she'd drunk that morning wasn't helping. Intending to sort out her options, she dropped onto the sofa, but couldn't keep her eyes open.

AN INSISTENT RINGING roused her from the depths of sleep. She reached out her hand to push the button on her alarm clock, and knocked something onto the floor.

Opening her eyes, she stared around the room, disoriented. This wasn't her bedroom. There were chairs and a fireplace. Bookcases. A coffee table.

She was in David's living room. Memories of the night before came flooding back. The phone was ringing. She picked it up off the floor and turned it on.

"Hello?" She hoped she sounded awake and together. Not like she'd just been sleeping on the couch.

"Is this Maddie Johnson?"

"Yes."

"My name is Frank Gervano, Ms. Johnson. I represent YourMarket, and I understand you have a piece of property available in Otter Tail."

YourMarket. They could undoubtedly pay more money than Quinn. Maddie's heart began to pound. "I do," she said, immediately alert. "Have you spoken to my Realtor? It's Laura Taylor. I can give you her number."

"I tried to call Ms. Taylor, but I couldn't get hold of her. Since I'm only in town for the day, I'd like to meet with you. I'm hoping we can do business."

"Any offers have to go through Laura."

"I'm not making any offers today," he assured her. "This would be very informal. I'd like to get a sense of your time frame, financing options, see if we can work together. That sort of thing."

A tiny voice told her "that sort of thing" should be handled by Laura. But maybe she could gauge how interested YourMarket was. How likely they were to make an offer. Something she could tell Hollis, so her friend wouldn't worry.

"I suppose it wouldn't hurt to meet you," Maddie said.

"Excellent. I noticed a small restaurant on Main Street. The Cherry Tree. Perhaps we could meet there."

"That's fine." She glanced at her watch. Noon. There would be a crowd. "I'm in the middle of something here, so how about in a couple of hours?"

There was a beat of silence. "Fine. I'll see you then, Ms. Johnson."

He didn't like waiting.

Too bad. She wasn't about to meet with a YourMarket representative during the lunch rush. In a couple of hours, the whole town would know about it.

Including Quinn.

She stood and shoved her hair behind her ears. So what? She didn't care what the people here thought. She didn't owe them anything. If the YourMarket people would pay her more than Quinn, the Harp was theirs.

She didn't owe Quinn anything, either.

She headed upstairs to shower and change her clothes.

THERE WERE ONLY A FEW customers in the Cherry Tree when she walked in two hours later. Jen appeared to be the only waitress.

"You still here? That's insane. You must have hardly slept last night."

"I'm almost done. I'll go home and sleep then. You having lunch?"

"Maybe a snack," she said. Her stomach rumbled at the fragrance of cinnamon and apples coming from the kitchen. "What smells so good?"

"Bernie's making pies. You want a slice?"

"Yes, thanks." Fifteen years ago, she wouldn't have ordered a piece of pie—she'd obsessed too much about her weight. Thank goodness she'd defeated that ogre. She nodded at the empty booth in the corner. "I'm, uh, meeting someone here. Okay if I take that booth?"

Jen's eyes twinkled. "Quinn? You two were pretty cozy this morning."

Jen had no idea how cozy they'd been; she was just fishing. "I'd locked myself out of the house, and he was getting me his extra key," Maddie said easily. "That's all."

"Uh-huh." She waved at the booth. "Go ahead. You probably need a cup of coffee, right?"

Amazing that she already knew how addicted Maddie was. "Yes, please."

After Jen set the coffee down, she pulled out her order pad. "Anything else besides the pie?"

Maddie's stomach was in a knot. "Just coffee."

"Got it." She shoved the order pad into her pocket. "Did I thank you for standing up for me with Quinn last night? I really appreciate it. It's not exactly what I want to do, but eventually I want to open a restaurant. Cooking for Quinn is a good first step."

"Did the two of you work something out? Are you going to keep on cooking?" Maddie asked.

"As much as I can. I don't want to quit here until…" Jen played with the order pad in her pocket. "Until we know for sure the Harp is going to be there."

"Yeah." As Jen hurried away, Maddie took a drink of coffee. Her hand shook as she set it down. Only because she'd had too much caffeine already today.

The bell over the door chimed and a man in an expensive business suit walked in. This had to be him. No one else in Otter Tail wore a suit, as far as she could tell, let alone on a Saturday.

She waved at him, and he strolled over. He was slick. City. Sophisticated.

So why was she instantly on guard? She was city, too.

"Ms. Johnson?" He stood next to the booth with his hand out. "Frank Gervano."

"Maddie," she said. She could feel the handful of customers in the restaurant watching them, but she didn't take her gaze off Gervano's face. "Have a seat."

# CHAPTER TEN

"WHAT DID YOU WANT to talk about, Mr. Gervano?" Maddie asked.

"It's Frank." He watched her closely. "How committed are you to selling your property, Ms. Johnson?"

*Careful. Guys like this can smell desperation.* "I know nothing about managing a pub, and I don't live in Otter Tail, so it would be foolish of me to keep the Harp. But I'm not in any hurry. I'll wait for the right offer."

"I see." He settled back against the cracked vinyl of the booth. "Our company would like to enter the market in Door County. Your property interests us. But we'd have to do a number of studies." He smiled. "Demographics. Traffic through town. That sort of thing."

His smile looked calculated.

"Of course."

Jen came over and slid a slice of apple pie onto the table in front of Maddie, then glanced at Gervano. "What can I get you?"

"A piece of that pie would be great," he said. "And water. Bottled, please."

"Sorry," Jen said. "We only have tap water."

"Really?" He frowned. "Then I guess I'll have tap water."

As she turned away, Jen rolled her eyes and shot Maddie a questioning look. Maddie took a sip of coffee.

"So, Frank. You're not in any hurry to buy, and I'm not in any hurry to sell. What are we doing here?"

Gervano's eyes flickered. "Getting acquainted, Maddie. I've found it's good business to know who you're dealing with."

"I agree. Tell me about YourMarket. How many local people would you be hiring for your store?"

"A new store generally brings approximately one hundred jobs," he said. Didn't really answer her question.

Jen put a piece of the apple pie, still steaming, in front of him. "Can I get you anything else?"

"Thanks, Jen, but I think we're set here," Maddie said.

"I'll leave this, then." She set the check on the table and walked away. Slowly, Maddie noticed.

"About your hiring policies," she pressed. "Do you hire from the community, or bring in your own employees?"

He gave her a tight smile. "We can't discriminate like that. It would be illegal to limit job applicants to one town only. But we do our best to hire locally."

So the answer was no. They probably brought in all the managers, then hired whoever would work most cheaply for the rest of the jobs. "What kind of sales tax revenue can a town expect to get from one of your stores?"

"That depends on the store, and the town, of course." Gervano took a bite of pie, then picked up his water glass. He studied it for a moment, as if making sure it was clean. "We have separate arrangements with each of our towns."

So YourMarket would be asking Otter Tail for tax incentives. Based on what she'd heard, Mayor Crawford would be more than happy to oblige. "What about traffic? How much additional traffic does a store usually bring?"

"For someone who doesn't live here, you seem quite concerned about the town," Gervano said.

"I may not live here, but I have history in this town," she said coolly. "My decision will affect a lot of people. I think they're legitimate questions."

"Absolutely." Gervano smiled, a piece of pastry stuck between his front teeth. "This is why I wanted to meet you. To learn about your concerns. Make sure we can address them."

"I appreciate that. About the traffic…?"

Gervano folded his hands on the table. "We pride ourselves in using sophisticated traffic pattern studies to place the entrances to our buildings." He cleared his throat. "But our stores are generally quite busy."

*Translation: not our problem.* Maddie's stomach churned. "I'm sure Laura Taylor could get you any information you might need about the town," she said.

"Have you gotten any other offers yet?"

"We have. Laura is considering them."

He raised his eyebrows. "More than one?"

"It's a valuable site. The Harp and Halo is a very successful business, and Otter Tail is becoming a tourist destination." She held his gaze. "I assume that's why YourMarket wants to locate here."

"You know the real estate business, I see."

Not well enough, or she wouldn't need to talk to him. "I know what questions to ask."

Gervano set his fork on his plate and glanced at his

watch. "It's been good talking with you, Maddie, but I have another appointment. I'll be in touch."

"With Laura," she said. "My Realtor."

"Of course." He squeezed out of the booth and picked up the check. "Thanks for your time."

As he walked up to the cash register, the door opened and Quinn stepped in. He froze when he saw Gervano, then watched as the YourMarket rep left the store.

Maddie wanted to slide down in the booth. Instead, she sat up taller. She had no reason to be ashamed that she'd met with Gervano.

"Hey, Quinn." Jen smiled despite her obvious fatigue. "You here for something to eat?"

"No, I came to ask if you'd be able to cook at the Harp tonight. But maybe it's way too much to put you through…."

"I've already worked a full shift here," she said. "But I could cook for a little while. How about until nine?"

"Anything would be a help," he said. "Thanks."

"I have some fresh pie, if you'd like a slice," Jen said. "Apple. Your favorite." She nodded her head in Maddie's direction. "Some company you might like, too."

Quinn's eyes met hers, and she saw him make the connection between her and Gervano. His expression hardened. "The pie sounds good, Jen."

He strode over to the booth and slid in across from her. "Gervano was here to meet with you, wasn't he?"

"Not your business," Maddie said, taking a bite of the now-tasteless pie.

"He wants the Harp, you know."

"There's a lot of that going around."

"Damn it, Maddie, he practically left a slime trail behind him when he walked out."

She hadn't liked Gervano any more than Quinn had. "His money is green. That's all that's important."

"Do you know what YourMarket would do to this town?" His voice was a harsh whisper, and the handful of people in the diner were now openly watching them. "It would destroy Otter Tail."

"Isn't that a little dramatic?" She kept her voice as low as his.

"YourMarket drives down the prices so local stores can't compete. It sucks the soul out of a community."

"Quinn, I know you don't want to lose the Harp. Believe me, I'd sell it to you if I could. But I have to sell it to whoever can give me the most money." For Hollis.

"So kissing me this morning didn't mean a thing."

"Keep your voice down," she said. "And if I recall, you were the one who started it." A horrible thought struck her. "Was that your way of trying to convince me to sell to you?"

"Of course not. You think I *wanted* to kiss you?" He closed his eyes. "Sorry, I didn't mean it that way."

It was too late. Memories flooded her, and remembered humiliation made her want to get far away from Quinn. "I'm glad we cleared that up," she said, sliding out of the booth. "Goodbye, Quinn."

She walked out of the Cherry Tree and didn't let herself look back.

QUINN FOUND HIMSELF watching the clock as 5:00 p.m. approached. Would Maddie show up for work? Or would she blow him off?

In her shoes, he probably wouldn't show. Not after what he'd said to her. As soon as the words were out of his mouth, he'd realized how they would hurt her. And that he'd lied. He *had* wanted to kiss her. Just didn't want to admit it.

The pub was already beginning to fill up, and people were watching the door expectantly. Clearly, everyone had heard about their conversation at the Cherry Tree. Or maybe they'd heard about the stop for coffee that morning. Either way, the crowd was looking to be entertained.

What had happened to his rules about not getting involved? About keeping his personal business private? His cool, detached lifestyle was crumbling around him. It had started the minute Maddie walked into the Harp that first night.

Even before seeing her in the Cherry Tree with Gervano, he'd spent the day trying to figure out what had happened earlier. Maddie was right—he'd made a move on her. Women had turned him down before. He'd always said "so long" and carried on. He never took it personally.

Because the women had never meant anything to him, he realized uneasily.

Maddie did. And that scared the hell out of him. So he'd overreacted. And hurt her in the process.

Then he'd gone and done it again at the Cherry Tree.

The door opened and Quinn tensed. But instead of Maddie, Sam Talbott and Annamae Simpson strolled in, arm in arm. Apparently, whatever Maddie had said to him had worked. Quinn rolled his eyes at the expression on Sam's face. The kid might as well have tiny hearts circling his head.

"So you guys are back together," he said.

"We are." Sam smiled idiotically down at Annamae. "Is Maddie here yet? I want to introduce her."

"Nope." Quinn concentrated on the glass he was filling with beer.

"When she gets here, tell her we're in the corner booth." He nuzzled Annamae's neck. "She's the one who made me realize that Annamae is my true love."

Quinn watched as Sam steered his girlfriend away from the bar. A few days ago, the kid had been slobbering all over Maddie. Now he was in love with Annamae again.

*True love.* Quinn snorted. *Yeah, right.* True lust was more like it.

He had no problem with lust—he liked it just fine. He had a little trouble with the whole true love concept.

"Hey, Quinn. What's up? You just eat something that tasted really bad?"

He yanked his gaze away from Sam and Annamae and watched Paul Black take a stool. "What are you doing here tonight?" he said, forcing a smile. "Didn't you get your fill last night?"

"The Harp is the place to be," his friend replied with a sly smile. "I'm expecting a good show tonight."

"You've heard Hank's band before. Do they have someone new playing with them?"

"I wasn't talking about the band."

"Oh, for God's sake. I thought you were an adult."

"I am. That's why I enjoy leisure activities with adult themes."

"Entertain this," Quinn said, flipping him a finger.

Paul laughed. "Give me a half-and-half to go along with my amusements, would you?"

"That drink is a pain in the ass." He filled a glass half-full with Harp beer, then grabbed a spoon and let Guinness flow over the back of it until the glass was full. "*You're* a pain in the ass, Paul."

"Then my job here is done." He took his beer and stood. "I like Maddie."

As Quinn stared at him, speechless, Paul wandered toward a group that included Delaney Spencer and Ian Hartshorn, a political science professor from Collier College over in Spruce Lake. Apparently, the gossip was bringing them in from miles around.

Quinn filled small bowls with pretzels and set them on the bar hard enough that they rattled. People here were supposed to be on *his* side. They were supposed to be helping him keep the Harp. Did they have any idea Maddie might sell the pub to YourMarket?

"So tell me about the new waitress, Quinn. I've been hearing a lot about her." Hank Martin, whose band was playing that evening, leaned against the bar, and Quinn reached to pull him a Guinness.

"You're here early, aren't you?" he asked.

"Nothing better to do." Hank sipped the dark beer.

As Quinn filled another order, the door opened. There was a beat of silence, then everybody began talking again.

Maddie hesitated in the doorway.

After a moment, she walked in, wearing the body-hugging green T-shirt and jeans she'd worn last night. As if she was coming to work. His heart began to pound.

"Is that her?" Hank asked in a low voice. "She's worth coming in early for."

He started toward Maddie, and Quinn reached across the bar and yanked him back. "Don't make me hurt you, buddy."

The musician slowly smiled. "Is that how it is?"

"You both work here. I don't want any drama."

"Whatever you say." He settled on a bar stool, looking at Quinn expectantly.

Maddie grabbed a clean apron, tied it on and disappeared into the growing crowd, ignoring him.

Quinn lost track of her for a while, but a few minutes later she returned to the bar and dropped off several drink orders. Before she could move away, he stepped in front of her, then herded her to a corner of the pub where no one could overhear them.

"I didn't expect you in tonight."

She raised her eyebrows. "You thought I'd leave you without a waitress? That would be bad for business. It might hurt the bottom line."

He saw pain, deep in her eyes. "I need to talk to you."

"I don't have time to chitchat. There are a lot of thirsty people out there." She hurried away without looking back. Just like she hadn't looked back as she left the Cherry Tree.

MADDIE DROPPED OFF another handful of orders and picked up the drinks Quinn had filled, then eased back into the crowd. She could feel Quinn's gaze boring holes in her back, but she ignored him.

She'd finished delivering the drinks and was taking

more orders when a man turned away from the group he was talking to and held up an empty glass. "Another Guinness, please."

"Sure." She scribbled it down, then reached for his glass. He held it just out of reach.

"You're the new waitress."

Wavy blond hair brushed his collar and framed a rugged face. When he smiled at her, a dimple flashed in his right cheek and his brown eyes twinkled. "Hank Martin," he said, holding out his hand. "My band is playing tonight."

"I'm Maddie," she said, relaxing. "I've heard good things about your group."

"We're not as good as Paul—but then, we don't have Delaney." He grinned. "We try harder, though."

"Can I get you something to eat?"

"No, thanks."

"Andre is gone. Jen Summers is cooking for us now."

"Really? Is she making something other than burgers and fish and chips?"

"How about a chicken wrap?"

"Excellent."

She wrote it on her pad and took his glass. "I'll get you another beer, too."

"How do you like working here?" Hank asked.

"It's fine." She plastered her professional smile on her face. "The people are great."

"Yeah, mostly." He nodded toward the bar. "Other than the boss. He just about took my head off a few minutes ago."

Maddie glanced over her shoulder to see Quinn

watching them. "No job is perfect," she said lightly. "Nice to meet you, Hank."

Once Hank's band started playing, the pub got more crowded, and it was easy to avoid Quinn. She dropped off the drink requests when he was busy with a customer at the bar, and picked them up when his attention was elsewhere.

She wasn't interested in going another round with him.

But in spite of her resolve, she knew every time he was watching her. His gaze touched the nape of her neck and drifted down her back, making her shiver. And she caught herself paying too much attention to him.

It infuriated her that she was still aware of him.

Her nerves were stretched taut and close to snapping when Jen touched her arm and murmured, "We have a problem."

# CHAPTER ELEVEN

"JEN!" A CUSTOMER JOSTLED Maddie's arm, and her tray dipped as she struggled to balance it. "What's wrong?"

Jen steadied the tray. "Do you have a minute?"

"Give me ten minutes to deliver these drinks and check the crowd one more time. I'm due for a break."

"Meet me in the kitchen," Jen said in a low voice.

A few minutes later, Maddie slipped through the swinging door and found Jen grilling a chicken breast and making a salad.

"Hey, Jen. What's up?"

The other woman paused, holding the knife she was using to chop a pear. "Martha told me you're selling the Harp to YourMarket."

Maddie's heart plummeted. She dropped her tray onto the stainless steel counter. "Why on earth would she say that?"

Jen held her gaze. "That guy you met at the diner. He was from YourMarket. He used his corporate credit card to pay his bill."

*Gervano was an idiot.* "He didn't even make me an offer, Jen. He just wanted to meet. That's it."

"But he's going to make an offer."

"I have no idea." The edge of the counter cut into her palms as she gripped it. "Please don't say anything to anyone else. And ask Martha not to, either. I don't want everyone angry at me."

"I won't say a word. Can't vouch for Martha, though. Nothing she likes as much as gossip."

"This gossip might hurt Quinn."

Jen turned the chicken on the grill. "Is that what you and Quinn were fighting about? You were in his truck at the crack of dawn, which was a positive development. Then this afternoon, I thought I'd have to hide the steak knives."

"'A positive development'? What's that supposed to mean?"

"It means Quinn has isolated himself in this pub ever since he opened it. He doesn't get involved, with anyone or anything." She smiled. "But maybe that's changed."

"Yeah, we're involved, all right. In a bad way. He wants to buy the Harp from me. And I can't afford to sell it to him. That's what we were fighting about."

Jen whistled. "That's ugly."

"Yeah."

"So what were you doing in his truck this morning? Negotiating?"

Maddie laughed, and some of her tension eased. She missed talking about stuff with Hollis and her other girlfriends.

"A raccoon got into the kitchen last night, and I freaked out. When I ran outside, I locked myself out of the house. Quinn came over to apologize—"

"After he left the pub at two."

"—and found me stranded. He had a key at his house. That's it."

Jen cut the chicken into strips and put it on the salad, then filled a small cup with what appeared to be home-made salad dressing. "He looked pretty worked up when he came into the Cherry Tree for coffee. Most people don't get that passionate about unlocking doors."

"Maybe there was other stuff, but it's over now."

"He was an idiot, wasn't he?"

Maddie sank onto the stool on the other side of the counter. "He was."

"It comes with the Y chromosome," Jen said. "He really is a good guy."

"That remains to be seen," Maddie muttered. "Was that it? Because I should deliver that salad."

"I wanted to tell you to be careful."

She frowned. "Quinn may be angry, but he's not going to do anything to me."

"Quinn would chew off his own hand before he hurt a woman," Jen said impatiently. "I wasn't talking about him."

"Then what?"

"One of my customers at the Cherry Tree told me he'd seen Andre at a bar in Fish Harbor. He was drunk, and he was going off on you and Quinn. He's pissed at Quinn for firing him and he blames you."

"He was threatening me?" Clearly, coming to Otter Tail had been a mistake on every front, Maddie thought, annoyed.

"Not in so many words. But you and Quinn better be careful. Andre has a temper."

"David's house has heavy-duty locks. I found that out last night," Maddie said. "I'll make sure I use them."

"You should have Quinn see you home after work, too."

"That's not going to happen," Maddie said quickly. She'd chew off her *own* hand before she asked Quinn for anything. "I can take care of myself."

"I'm going to tell Quinn about Andre, too."

"Absolutely tell him Andre was talking smack. He needs to know. But don't you dare say anything about me. If you do, I'll—I'll…" She shoved her hands into her pockets. "I don't know what I'll do, but it'll be messy and it will involve pain."

A smile flickered at the corners of Jen's mouth. "Quinn's a smart guy. He's going to figure it out. He'll know Andre was talking about you, too."

"If he's so smart, why was he such an ass?"

"You should be asking me that." Quinn's voice. Behind her.

She spun around. "Eavesdropping?"

"Looking for you. I noticed you'd disappeared."

"I was taking a break." She lifted her chin. "Do I need your permission now to go to the bathroom?"

"I'll deliver this salad," Jen said, sidling past her and Quinn. "You two have fun." She pushed through the swinging door, leaving them alone.

"If you're searching for the bathroom, you're in the wrong place," Quinn said.

"Then I must have taken a wrong turn."

She tried to walk past him, but he stopped her with

a hand to her arm. "You're right. I *was* an ass, and I apologize. Okay?"

"For what? There are so many things to choose from."

A muscle in his jaw twitched. "For the way I acted at my house. And for what I said at the Cherry Tree."

"Fine." She stepped around him. "I need to get back to work."

"Wait." He put his hand on her shoulder, and she stilled. His touch made her shiver, and she hated that.

"I lost it when I saw you with Gervano. But it wasn't just about him buying the Harp. There's something off about that guy, and I was worried about you."

Maddie rolled her eyes. "And you would know this because you didn't like the way he looked?"

"Okay, I was pissed because he wants to buy the Harp, and you were listening to him. I'll cop to that. But there's more to it."

Maddie jerked her head toward the other room. "As much as I'd like to have a heart-to-heart, there are a bunch of people out there who want drinks. They're going to get testy if we're back here baring our souls instead of serving their beers." This time he didn't stop her. "Bad timing, Quinn."

The story of her life.

SEVERAL PEOPLE SIGNALED her for drinks as soon as Maddie came out of the kitchen. She took a deep breath. Okay, she could do this. She could hide her feelings, smile and be friendly. Tomorrow night would be easier. And the next night easier still.

She couldn't quit. Quinn was a jerk and she'd be

happy to forget all about him, but it wasn't that simple. He'd lose a lot of money if he didn't have a waitress. And so would she.

So she'd stick around. As long as the Harp stayed busy, it would be easy to avoid Quinn.

Not so easy to ignore the nerves that jumped when she felt him watching her. Or when she caught a glimpse of him.

A young couple close by waved her over. "What can I get you?" she asked.

"Two beers, please," the young man said. His eyes didn't quite meet hers.

"Can I see your IDs?" Maddie asked.

The girl rummaged in her large purse for her wallet. But when she held her driver's license out to Maddie, her hand shook.

"Here's mine." The guy placed his on top of hers.

Maddie studied his license. He'd just turned twenty-one a couple of weeks earlier. The picture wasn't great, but it was recognizable.

Then she examined the other license. The girl in the picture had hair down to her shoulders. The one in front of her wore a ponytail, so it was hard to judge the length of her hair. Eye color on the license was blue, but in the dimly lit bar, her eyes seemed dark. When Maddie glanced up, the girl shifted on the seat.

"Sandy, when's your birthday?" Maddie asked.

She looked like a deer caught in the headlights. "Um, February 21."

Maddie tucked the licenses into a pocket of her apron. "I have to give these to the bartender."

The boy jumped up, almost knocking over the chair. "Hey, you don't want our business, fine. Give me the licenses and we'll leave."

"Sorry, can't do that."

The girl's eyes filled with tears and she pressed her hand to her mouth. "Jesse, make her give them back."

"You'll have to deal with the bartender if you want them," Maddie said quietly.

After staring at her for a moment, Jesse squared his shoulders. "Okay. You stay here, Carrie. This is my fault, so I'll handle it."

"Why don't you two sit tight for a minute?" Maddie said, feeling sorry for the terrified girl and the boy who was willing to take the blame. "Let me talk to him first."

"Okay." The kid sank back, relieved.

After making sure that no one's glass was empty, she made her way to the bar. Quinn was serving Hank, and the two men were smiling about something. She stood at the far end and waited to snag his attention.

Hank nodded in her direction and said something to Quinn with a grin. Quinn's smile faded as he headed toward her. "What can I do for you?"

"For starters, lighten up. People are supposed to have fun in here. Smile, Quinn. At least act as if we like each other."

One corner of his mouth quirked up. "Maybe the problem is there's too much of that 'like' thing going on. What do you have?"

*Too much like going on?* Struggling to hide her disbelief, she pulled out the two driver's licenses and nodded toward the young couple. "She tried to use this ID to buy a beer. It's not hers."

He studied the kids. "I don't know them. They're not from Otter Tail." He glanced at the ID and frowned. "Bring them into the office."

"Wait a minute." Maddie put her hand on his wrist, taking it away immediately when his muscles tensed.

"What?"

"The girl is scared to death. Don't be too hard on her."

His expression hardened. "I *want* to scare those kids. I want to scare them so bad they don't think about committing a crime ever again."

"The guy is legal. It's the girl whose ID is fake."

"Are you telling me he didn't know she was using someone else's license?"

"He knew. But he was willing to take the blame."

"He's a real stand-up guy, all right. Don't try to defend them, Maddie. They broke the law. I *should* call the police. Instead, I'm just going to scare the crap out of them."

"Are you always so black-and-white?"

"You bet. There isn't a lot of gray when it comes to breaking the law."

"There's always room for compassion."

"For some things, yeah. Not for this." He tossed the rag onto the counter. "I'm not going to debate this with you tonight. This is how I handle underage drinkers. If you have a better idea, we can discuss it sometime when we're not working."

"Fine. I'll show them to your office."

She walked back to the young couple, who watched

her with worried expressions. "You can see Mr. Murphy in his office."

The girl shrank closer to the guy. "I want to go home."

"You're free to go. But you won't get your driver's licenses back unless you talk to him."

"It'll be okay, Carrie," the guy said, putting his arm around her.

"Follow me," Maddie said.

The pub quieted as everyone watched them. Apparently most of them knew what it meant when a kid went into Quinn's office.

Maddie stayed with them until Quinn arrived. He nodded at her, then closed the door behind her.

"Quinn is right, you know." Patrick O'Connor sat in his usual spot at the end of the bar. "I was a high school teacher. You have to be firm with young adults."

"He's not going to cut them any slack, that's for sure." Maddie listened to the rumble of Quinn's voice behind the door and was thankful she wasn't on the receiving end of his lecture.

Sam Talbott waved, and she went over to the booth he shared with Annamae. They sat close together on the same side, Sam's arm around Annamae's waist. Maddie smiled. At least she'd done something right in Otter Tail.

"Hey, Maddie," Sam said happily. "I need another Bud Light. And Annamae needs more iced tea."

"Coming right up," Maddie said as she scribbled the order. She nodded toward Quinn's office. "Do you know those two kids?"

"Nope. They're not from around here," Annamae said. "They're probably tourists. Quinn gets fake IDs every week during the summer. None of the kids ever come back."

"I hope they don't just go somewhere else," Maddie said with a glance at the still-closed office door.

"I'm guessing they don't," Sam said. "He used to give them the talk in the bar, where everyone could listen. He always told them he was going to e-mail their license pictures to every bar in Door County so they couldn't try to drink anywhere else."

She shouldn't have argued with Quinn about his method, Maddie realized. Public humiliation was painful, but it was better than having a car wreck.

Ten minutes later the couple followed Quinn out of the office. The girl was crying, the boy pale-faced and grim. They hurried to the door and left.

"Another kid with a fake ID bites the dust," Hank said behind her. "Put another notch on the bar."

Maddie spun around. "It's not a joking matter. I'm glad he takes it seriously."

"Whoa!" The musician held up his hands. "I wasn't criticizing." He gave her a slow smile. "Pretty passionate defense of him, Maddie."

"Why wouldn't I defend him?" she answered, struggling to regain her composure. It was stupid to let Hank agitate her. "He's right."

"Let's just say I sensed a disturbance in the force between the two of you tonight."

"What's that supposed to mean?" Maddie asked, staring him down.

"You were in his truck at six-thirty this morning. Tonight it's all good lovin' gone bad."

"I have no idea what you're talking about." She nodded toward the front of the pub. "Don't you have music to play? You were supposed to start ten minutes ago."

"Nag, nag, nag," he said, shaking his head. "You're as bad as Quinn." He ambled toward the area where two other musicians were tuning their instruments.

As she went to the end of the bar to pick up her orders, Quinn glanced up from the drink he was mixing. "You going to yell at me for making that girl cry?"

"Of course not. You were right." Maddie sighed. "The girl gave me those scared, weepy eyes and I felt sorry for her. I wasn't thinking of the big picture."

Quinn was silent as Maddie lifted the round tray. His expression was unreadable. "What?" she said.

He shook his head. "You don't fight fair, Maddie." Then he walked the other way, carrying the drink he'd made.

IT WAS STILL A COUPLE OF hours until closing time, and Maddie's face was sore from all the smiling. There were a lot of people in the Harp she hadn't met before tonight, and most of them had introduced themselves and told her how fond they'd been of David. They'd asked her opinion of Otter Tail and welcomed her to town.

They'd been friendly and pleasant, so she was certain they hadn't heard about YourMarket yet. All the warm fuzzies would disappear when they did.

Hank and his band were still playing and the pub was still packed. As she wove through the crowd, three bottles of beer on her tray, she glanced at the empty stool at the end of the bar. Patrick had already left. Maybe she'd take a quick break, even if it meant watching Quinn work. She had tried to avoid him all evening, but was too tired now to care.

As she headed toward the two men and a woman waiting for the beers, someone tugged on her arm from behind. Masking the irritation she felt when a customer touched her, she turned around with a smile. "Can I help…" She saw who it was and took a step back. "J.D. Did you want something?"

"Yeah," he said. "Get me a draft." His eyes glittered, and Maddie realized with a sinking stomach that the Harp wasn't his first stop of the night.

She nodded. "As soon as I deliver these drinks."

"Crystal would have got it right away." For a moment, she read bewilderment in his brown eyes.

"Sorry. Crystal's not here, J.D.," she said. Had the former waitress dumped him? Was that why he was drowning his sorrows? "I'll only be a minute or two."

Five minutes later she returned with a cola. "It's on the house, J.D." She smiled. "You need to pace yourself."

"I don't drink that shit. I want a beer." He knocked the glass from the tray, spilling the cola on her. The liquid was a sudden splash of cold through her jeans and T-shirt.

Maddie stared at the broken glass on the floor and her wet clothes. "That's what I get for trying to be nice to you? Leave, J.D. Right now."

"You going to make me, city girl?"

"You bet I am."

Quinn moved her aside. "Get out of here, J.D. And don't bother to come back. I tried to cut you some slack after what happened with Crystal, but we're done. You're on the list. For good."

J.D. stepped closer, his eyes glazed. "You think you can throw me out, Murphy? You think you're tough enough?"

"I don't need to be tough," Quinn said. "You're too drunk to put up a fight."

"You think so?" J.D.'s sorrow had morphed into rage and a violence Maddie recognized. She'd seen it in some of the people she'd interviewed during her career as a reporter.

Seeing J.D. about to throw a punch, she stepped between the two men. The blow glanced off the side of her face.

And knocked her to the floor.

## CHAPTER TWELVE

THE SUDDEN SILENCE in the Harp cut through Maddie's haze of pain and disbelief. Even the band faltered to a stop.

Quinn knelt beside her. "Maddie? Are you okay?" His hand was gentle as he touched her cheek. "Paul, get some ice."

"I…I think so," she said, dazed. Her butt was cold and wet from the cola, her face throbbed and her head was spinning.

Quinn put his arm around her shoulders and lifted her up, then guided her to a booth. An older woman eased her onto the seat and brushed her hair away from her face. "Hurry up with that ice, Paul," she called.

"I'm going to kick your ass into the middle of next week, J.D.," Maddie heard Quinn say. His voice was cold and flat. "And I'll enjoy doing it."

"Back off, Quinn." Brady Morgan, a regular patron she recognized as a Door County deputy sheriff, elbowed him aside. "I'll take care of him. Stroger, you're under arrest."

A chair toppled over as J.D. struggled briefly. In seconds, Brady had him on the floor and handcuffed with a white flex cuff he pulled out of his pocket. Then he yanked J.D. to his feet. "This was my night off, you son of a bitch. Now I'm going to be doing paperwork until the crack of dawn. Assault, battery, resisting arrest, property damage. And a few more I'll think of later. Let's go. The cavalry is here."

Maddie heard the sound of a siren in the distance, then saw the flashing lights of a police car in front of the pub. Moments later, Brady was heading for the door, shoving J.D. ahead of him.

"What were you thinking, Maddie?" Quinn crouched next to her. "You stepped right into that punch."

The whole left side of her face ached with bone-deep pain and she felt oddly detached, as if Quinn was speaking to her from the end of a tunnel. "I knew he was going to hit you. I thought he'd stop if I got in the way."

"What kind of dumb-ass thinking was that?" He cupped her cheek. "He could have broken your jaw."

Laura Taylor stepped between them. "Let me see." She ran her fingers over Maddie's face, pressing gently on her cheek and jaw. "I don't think anything's broken."

"Is this part of your service as my Realtor?" Maddie asked.

"I used to be an EMT."

"Here's the ice." Paul elbowed his way through the crowd and handed Quinn a plastic bag. Then he looked at Laura. "Why are you still here? I thought you went to bed at nine o'clock."

"Go screw yourself, Paul," she said pleasantly. Then she walked away.

Startled, Maddie watched Laura retreat as Quinn held the bag in place. The cold burned, but after a moment, it eased the pain in her cheek.

"Get out of the way, all of you," the older woman who'd been in the booth said. "Give the girl some breathing room." She waited until everyone began moving away, then turned to Maddie. "I'm Sue Schmidt. Give me that ice pack, Quinn. I'll help her with it."

"Thanks, but I've got it," he answered.

"You've got a pub to run," Sue said. "Go do it."

There was a moment of tense silence. Finally, he said, "Yes, ma'am." He leaned around the older woman to look Maddie in the eye. "I'll be back in a few minutes."

Wishing he had stayed, Maddie watched out of her right eye as he walked away. Her left eye was swollen almost shut.

Sue slid into the seat beside her and took the ice bag. "I taught Quinn when he was in eighth grade, and he was a handful even then. You have to speak sternly to him." She eased the ice off Maddie's face for a moment. "You're going to have a bruise. But I think you'll avoid a black eye."

*Speak sternly to Quinn?* Maddie hid her smile and sat up straight, taking the bag away from the woman. "Thanks. The ice is helping. I've got it now."

Sue nodded. "I'll find you a glass of water."

As she hurried away, others came by, asking if she was okay. Paul leaned in and said, "I think you went above and beyond the call of duty." He studied her cheek. "J.D. better watch out. I've never seen Quinn in a rage before. It's pretty scary."

Maddie set the ice on the table. "He better not do anything stupid."

Paul shook his head. "He's way beyond stupid. He's into dangerously hormonal territory."

"Oh, for God's sake," Maddie said. She moved her jaw from side to side experimentally, and the pain wasn't bad. More like a dull ache now. "J.D. wasn't trying to hit me."

"But he did," Paul said quietly. "Quinn is entitled to be angry."

Maddie glared at him, although she was afraid the effect was lessened by the fact that she could only use one eye. "Entitled? What's that supposed to mean?"

"This is his place, and a patron assaulted an employee." He raised his eyebrows. "What did you think I meant?"

"Oh. Right."

Paul's eyes twinkled as he stepped away, and she stood slowly. The room tilted to one side, then righted. "I'm ready to go back to work."

"You're going to sit back down and stay there until I get my car," Sue said briskly, setting a glass of water on the table. "Then I'm driving you home."

"I can't do that," Maddie said. The pub was still crowded, and no one was about to leave. They'd be talking about the drama for days. "I have to work." She looked toward the bar, where Quinn was filling orders as he kept an eye on her. "I'm the only waitress."

Sue scoffed. "What do you think he did before you started working here? He'll be fine. Now sit down."

She turned to leave, apparently believing that Maddie would obey her. Instead, Maddie made her way to the bar. Quinn hurried to intercept her.

"What are you doing? Sit down." He skimmed his finger over the bruise, and his expression darkened. "J.D. is going to be sorry he was born."

"It's fine, Quinn," she said firmly. "It hardly even hurts anymore."

"I can't believe Sue let you leave that booth."

"She went to get her car. She says she's driving me home, but I told her I wanted to work."

"She's right," he said. "You should go home and take care of that bruise. Put your feet up and ice it." He smiled. "You can try saying no to Sue, but you won't win."

"Yeah, she's a little intimidating."

"Not once you get to know her," he said quietly. "She did a lot for me."

"She said the secret to handling you is to speak sternly. I'll have to remember that."

"There are other ways to handle me."

Before Maddie could answer, one of the regulars, a burly man with blond hair, put his hand on her shoulder. "You okay, Maddie? You need boxing lessons if you're going to take on J.D. I'll teach you how to punch back."

*Good God.* "Thanks, uh…"

"Augie. Augie Weigand."

"Thank you, Augie. But I'm not planning on getting into a boxing match with J.D."

"We'll watch out for you. If he comes in here again, we'll take care of him."

"Thank you," Maddie said, touched. "That's very thoughtful."

"We watch out for our own."

She was speechless as Augie walked away. "What did he mean?" she finally asked Quinn.

"You live here. You work here. Of course you're one of us."

"But...I'm not staying. I'm going back to Chicago."

"No one knows that," he said.

Pleasure whispered through her. *One of them.* She'd never been part of a *them* before. One of a community.

It wasn't going to last long, she reminded herself. Only until she sold the Harp to YourMarket. Then, no one in Otter Tail was going to be asking her how she was doing. No one was going to be offering to hold an ice bag on her cheek, or teach her how to box.

Sue Schmidt came bustling in the door, frowning as she spotted Maddie. "You're supposed to be sitting down," she said. She turned to Quinn. "I'm taking her home. She needs to get off her feet."

"Thanks, Sue," Quinn said. "I appreciate it."

Sue nodded. "I know."

Moments later, Maddie was standing in front of Sue's new sedan. "I can't get in your car," she said. "My pants are soaked. I don't want to get cola on your upholstery."

"Not a problem." The woman opened the trunk and pulled out a thin blanket. "Sit on this."

As they drove toward David's house, Maddie said, "I'm a stranger. I'm here to sell the Harp. How come you're all being so nice to me?"

"You'll do the right thing," Sue said. She glanced at Maddie. "I can tell."

"I appreciate the vote of confidence, but what's right for me might not be right for the town. I have a lot of debts to pay off."

The other woman frowned. "Hmm. That's a problem."

"It is." Where would all the people gather, once the Harp was gone?

"You'll think of something."

Too bad Maddie wasn't so confident. Hollis's phone call earlier had reminded her of what was at stake.

Now she had the town of Otter Tail, as well as Hollis, waiting for her decision.

LATER THAT EVENING, Quinn stood on the porch of David's house and jammed his hands in his pockets. Would Maddie even want to see him after the way he'd treated her earlier that day?

It was after midnight, but he had to talk to her. Make sure she was okay. The sight of her head jerking back, of her dropping to the floor, was replaying in an endless loop in his brain.

The light was on in the kitchen, so she was awake.

He rang the doorbell before he could change his mind.

After a few moments, she peered out the window at the side of the door, then the dead bolt clicked and the door opened. "Quinn. What are you doing here?"

He couldn't read her expression in the darkness. Was she glad to see him? Or did she want him to leave? "I needed to make sure you were okay."

"Come on in." She wore red plaid pajama pants and a white T-shirt that read Jesus Hates The Yankees.

"I didn't know you were a baseball fan."

"Of course I am. I live in Chicago."

"We may have to reassess this…friendship. I'm a Brewers' fan."

"That bunch of losers and their sausage races?"

His lips twitched. She couldn't be suffering too much if she could talk smack like that. "How's the face?"

She shrugged. "I'll live."

He put his hand at her waist, and the heat of her skin through the thin shirt burned him. When they reached the kitchen, he held her chin and studied the ugly purple bruise on the left side of her face.

"Damn it!"

"It looks worse than it feels," she said. "I've been icing it, and it's pretty numb."

He cupped her cheek, wishing he could absorb the bruise into his hand and get rid of her pain. "Did you take any painkillers?"

"I took ibuprofen. And—I know I shouldn't combine the two, but I don't care—I'm having some wine." She eased away from him and reached for a bottle of red on the counter. "Would you like a glass?"

So she wasn't going to throw him out. "No, thanks. Why don't we sit down so you can keep icing?"

"Can I get you anything to drink first?"

"I'm good. If I want something, I know where everything is." He hesitated. "Or at least where it used to be."

She headed out to the screened porch. "Nothing's changed," she said, sitting on the couch there.

*Oh, yes, it had.*

When it was David's house, Quinn had spent hours here, drinking coffee, talking about politics, books and life. Getting sober.

He'd been as comfortable here as he'd been at his own place.

There was nothing comfortable about this porch now.

He sat on one of the chairs, an arm's length away from Maddie. Her scent drifted toward him on the lake breeze, and he remembered the sweet taste of her mouth.

Her soft curves, pressed against him.

The tiny sounds she'd made as she kissed him.

"I shouldn't have come over here," he said, starting to rise. "I'm disturbing you."

She gazed at him over the rim of her wineglass, and met his eyes. "No. You're not," she said.

"Yeah, well, I'm disturbing myself," he muttered.

"Why is that, Quinn?"

Her voice sounded low and throaty. Seductive. It made his hands itch to touch her. "I should let you get some sleep," he said desperately.

Finally she broke their gaze. "You spent a lot of time here with David?" She took another sip of wine, then set the glass down.

*David.* That was a safer topic. "Yeah, I did. He was my friend. My best friend." Which was why the betrayal still hurt.

She tucked her legs beneath her. "I'm sorry."

"Doesn't matter now."

"It does. It was wrong of him to break his promise."

Quinn didn't want his bitterness to come spewing out. He didn't want her to know how petty and resentful he was. "He told me you worked for the *Chicago Herald.* What kind of reporting do you do?"

"Investigative." She picked up her glass and stared into the dark wine. "Then there were layoffs. None of the other papers were hiring—they were all in the middle of layoffs, too."

"Is that why you need to sell the pub?"

"No, that's entirely my own stupidity." She took a deep breath. "I got a buyout when I left the *Herald*. I invested the money in real estate, thinking I could renovate houses and make a profit while I looked for another newspaper job."

"But you didn't make a profit."

"No." She sighed. "I got in way over my head. I started out doing a lot of the work myself, but it was taking longer than I'd planned. I couldn't find another newspaper job, the housing market collapsed and I ran out of money. Now I owe a lot of people, including my best friend, who lent me money from her IRA."

"You didn't know house-flipping is risky? That you can lose a lot of money, really fast?"

She stood abruptly. "Of course I knew. I just enjoy throwing my money into a bottomless hole." She walked into the kitchen and came back with the bottle of wine and another glass. "If I'm going to spill my secrets, I don't want to drink alone."

"No, thanks. I don't drink anymore."

"I'm sorry." She nudged the glass toward the other end of the table. "I shouldn't have offered again."

"How would you know?" He shrugged. "I used to drink. That's why I wanted to open the Harp. I figured if I was going to drink, I might as well make it pay for me."

"Looks like it has," she answered, equally lightly.

She'd opened up to him, told him about her mistakes. The least he could do was give her an honest answer. "I was an angry drunk when I came home to Otter Tail," he said. "David helped me quit. He told me he wouldn't lease The Office to me if I kept drinking. I'd spent a lot of time in an Irish pub in Milwaukee. Too much, but I remembered how welcoming it was. I knew everyone in that place. Otter Tail needed somewhere for people to get together, and I wanted to transform The Office into a pub. So I quit. Even then, David was afraid it would be too hard, being around alcohol every night. But I was determined."

"Testing yourself?"

"I figured if I could work around booze all night, pretty soon I wouldn't want it anymore."

"Is it working?"

"Sometimes."

"Sorry." She snatched up the two glasses and the bottle of wine and stood to take them back to the kitchen. "I wouldn't have had the wine if I'd known."

He took the glass she'd been using and set it down on the table. "Don't apologize for drinking in front of me. People drink in front of me at the Harp all the time."

"That's business."

"If you want the wine, Maddie, drink it. You're not going to damage my fragile psyche. Watching you drink a glass of wine isn't going to make me start drinking again."

"It feels rude," she said. "Like smoking in front of someone who's trying to quit. Or eating a hot fudge sundae with someone who's on a diet."

He raised his eyebrows. "Stubborn, aren't you?"

"World class."

"I'll make a note of that." He settled back in the chair. "It always pays to know your opponent."

# CHAPTER THIRTEEN

MADDIE LEANED TOWARD HIM over the arm of the couch, and her T-shirt pulled taut against her chest. "Is that what we are? Opponents?"

He forced his gaze to her face and away from her nipples, straining against the fabric. "What do you want to be?"

"I'm not sure, Quinn." She flopped back against the couch, and her voice was soft in the darkness. "Friends, maybe? At least not enemies."

"For a while, I thought we were more than friends."

"Hard for two people to be friends, let alone more, if they don't know each other."

He made it a rule to keep himself isolated from other people. Even from the women he dated. It was easier that way. No risk. No pain.

No chance of the kind of disappointment that would lead him back to the bottle.

Weak light streamed through the kitchen windows and framed the red-gold of her hair. Moonlight bleached the floor a ghostly white, but the rest of the porch was shadowed and mysterious.

"What do you want to know about me?" he asked.

"Whatever you'd like to tell me."

He stood and paced the small porch. "I moved to Milwaukee after high school and joined the police force." He knew the dimensions of this room exactly: ten feet by eleven. He'd memorized every crack, every uneven spot in the tile floor.

He'd done plenty of pacing here when he was trying to stop drinking.

"Did you like being a cop?"

He stopped and stared out at the night, barely noticing the full moon. In the breeze, the fresh smell of lake water swirled around him.

"At first I did. I thought I was doing something worthwhile. Something important. Helping people."

"But…"

He turned to pace again. "I started to hate it. The brutality, the misery, the callousness. The ugly things people do to one another. That's when I started taking my drinking seriously."

"Come sit down, Quinn." Maddie held out a hand, and he took it, allowing her to pull him down beside her.

She twined their fingers together and pressed her palm to his. Reassurance? Comfort? Sympathy? He had no idea. But he held her hand as if he was drowning and she could pull him to safety.

"Why did you quit?"

He stared into the darkness, seeing the squalid alley. Seeing Donyell's body, crumpled and bloody next to the stinking Dumpster. "I had an informant. A kid. Sixteen. He was a gang member, but he wanted out, and I was trying to set him up with a place in a safer neighborhood. I told him to call me anytime if he needed help."

Maddie shifted until their bodies were touching. "What happened?"

"It was my day off, and I was drunk. Passed out. He called my cell, but I didn't hear it. The next thing I knew, my partner was banging on my door. They'd found Donyell in an alley. Dead. He'd been shot."

"And you blame yourself."

"It was my fault." Quinn wanted to move away from her comfort, but he needed it too badly. "If I hadn't been drunk, I'd have saved him. I'd have made sure he was safe."

"You don't know that," she said softly. "You have no idea whether you could have helped him or not. No idea if you could have gotten there in time."

"Yeah, well, I didn't have a chance to find out." He stood again, staring out sightlessly. "I was drunk."

He heard her rise, then she slipped her arms around his waist. "I'm sorry, Quinn." Her breath was warm against his back. "That's a horrible burden to carry."

"I quit the force and came back home." He'd spent the first month drunk. He would have spent the second month drunk, as well, but David had found him one night in The Office.

"David saved me," he said quietly. "Maybe that's why he didn't let me buy the pub. Maybe he thought I'd start drinking again if he wasn't around to rein me in."

"You know that's not true," she said. She moved around him and grabbed his shoulders. "David believed in second chances, and so do I."

"If he was such a believer in second chances, why didn't he give me a second chance? Why didn't he make sure I got the pub?"

"I have no idea. But he always kept his promises to me. If David was your friend, he believed in you. He trusted you. That I *do* know."

Then why hadn't David sold him the pub? It was the only thing Quinn wanted.

At least in the long term. Short term, he had a few other ideas.

"Enough about me," he said, standing perfectly still. "I came to make sure you were all right, not spill my guts."

"I'm glad you did."

"Why is that?"

Her mouth was a tempting curve as she said, "Because now I know who I'm kissing." She cupped his face in her hands and urged his mouth down to hers.

He couldn't move for a moment, then gathered her close. She was tender where he was harsh. He had no business getting involved with her. But her silky hair curled around his fingers, and he kissed her back.

He tasted the corner of her mouth, trailed his tongue along the seam of her lips. He wanted to plunge inside, to taste the sweet warmth that had obsessed him since the last time he'd kissed her.

Wrapping her arms around his neck, she swayed against him. His legs suddenly unsteady, he scooped her into his arms and stumbled back to the couch. He fell onto it and held her across his lap.

Her breasts pressed against his chest as his mouth moved over hers. She clung to him as he urged her lips open and stroked her tongue. The tiny noise she made in the back of her throat made him groan.

Wild to touch her, he ran his hand down her arm. Her skin was as soft as the lake water, cool and smooth. When she arched her spine, her breast grazed his hand, and he brushed it with his thumb.

"Quinn." She speared her fingers through his hair, and held his mouth to hers. When he moved his hand away from her breast, she caught it in hers and guided it back. "Please don't stop."

She smelled like the night, dark and mysterious. More alluring than any whiskey. And beneath that, he could taste her musky desire. He fumbled with the hem of her top and felt her warm back.

"Are you trying to drive me crazy with these T-shirts?" he muttered as he worked his hand beneath the pajama bottoms and cupped her hip. The flannel trapped his hand, so he couldn't explore her curves. "I want to see you."

He felt her smile against his mouth. "You, too." She tugged at his shirt, pulling it out of his pants, then burrowed beneath it. She smoothed her fingers over his muscles, exploring, then combed through the hair on his chest. She rubbed her thumb over his flat male nipple, and the sensation shot straight to his groin.

"Stop, Maddie," he whispered, his hands gliding over her curves until he was holding her breasts.

"Why?" she murmured.

He lifted her off his lap, then stood, pulling her close as he walked her backward toward the kitchen. "That couch was too small. We need to go upstairs. Find a bed."

She bumped into the island as he steered her through

the kitchen, and her apron from the Harp fell on the floor. Coins spilled onto the tiles and rolled in circles. He felt the exact moment she regained her senses. She stiffened and edged away from him.

"Bed?"

"We've moved on to the action part of the program." He nudged the apron away with the toe of his shoe and pulled her against him. "I want you, Maddie."

Her mouth opened beneath his.

But then a shudder rippled through her, and she moved back from him as if she were tearing a part of herself away. Even in the moonlight, he could see the flush on her face.

"I'm sorry," she said. "I shouldn't have kissed you."

His body disagreed. Strongly. He closed his eyes for a moment, trying to regain some control. Finally, when he was sure he wouldn't beg, he released a breath. "You're right. I don't want your pity."

She put her hand over his mouth. "Pity had nothing to do with what I…wanted." She fumbled to straighten her twisted T-shirt, but her hands were shaking. "I guess I shouldn't have had the wine on top of the ibuprofen."

He pushed her hands away and tugged the shirt down over her hips, then gripped her there.

"Bad timing," she said, watching his hands on her body.

"The worst." He let her go and stepped away. "I'm still going to stay here tonight, okay?"

She stared at him. "No, it's not okay. Bad idea, remember?"

"I'll stay in David's room. I want to make sure you're

all right." He let himself touch her hair again. "That you don't have a concussion or something."

"I'm fine, Quinn." She cupped the bruise on her face. "I didn't feel a thing when you were kissing me."

"Really? I'll have to work on my technique, then."

She smiled. "I meant the bruise. I felt plenty everywhere else. I'll be fine."

"I want to stay, Maddie," he said quietly. "I feel responsible. I should have headed J.D. off earlier. I should have made sure he didn't get a chance to punch you."

"That's crazy talk. It's my own fault. I stepped in front of him."

"Yeah, but I won't be able to sleep if I go home. So I'm going to stay."

"Why won't you take no for an answer?"

"Because I'm just as stubborn as you are."

HE WATCHED MADDIE SHUT the door to the frilly, girlie bedroom, then he walked into David's room. Quinn had been in here only a few times, all since David's death, but sadness overtook him as he looked around.

David was everywhere—from the full bookcases that lined the walls to the pieces of sea glass clustered on his dresser to the walking stick propped behind the door.

Quinn was still pissed off at David for not keeping his promise. But as he stared around the bedroom, he just missed his friend.

Quinn found a new toothbrush in the bathroom and a dried-up tube of toothpaste. He managed to brush his teeth and strip out of his clothes, then opened the window and fell into bed.

Cool air drifted into the room, bringing with it the tangy scent of Lake Michigan. Maddie must have opened her window, too, because the soft sounds that floated into his room drove him crazy.

He lay in bed, imagining what the sounds meant. The metallic click was her earrings and necklace being laid on the dresser. The slide of wood on wood was a drawer opening. The soft whisper of fabric was Maddie undressing.

Groaning, he rolled over and pulled the pillow over his head. A picture of Maddie was lodged in his brain and he couldn't get it out. Her lush breasts, hidden only by the shirt, her nipples tight with arousal against the thin material. Her mouth, lips swollen, moving over his chest. Her red hair caressing his skin.

"Damn it." He rolled onto his back, uncomfortable and aching for her.

He was an idiot. But he closed his eyes and imagined he could hear her sliding between the sheets of the bed next door.

It was going to be a long night.

HE AWAKENED TO THE SOUND of footsteps below. For a confused moment he thought it was morning and time to get up. But moonlight still poured into the room. David's room.

There was someone downstairs.

Andre? Quinn had heard about the former employee's threats.

He jumped out of bed and grabbed his jeans as he

opened the door. He didn't see any lights downstairs. But he heard someone moving around.

Grabbing David's walking stick from behind the door, he crept down the stairs. The intruder was in the kitchen now. Quinn studied the shadows. Wondered where the bastard was hiding. Gripping the walking stick more tightly, he edged toward the kitchen.

Whoever was there must be holding still, because Quinn couldn't make out any movement in the moonlight-dappled room. Had the intruder gone out the back door?

He eased inside, every sense on alert. Someone was close by. As he circled the island, he saw a flash of movement on the screened porch.

What the hell was an intruder doing out there? There was nothing on the small porch but the couch, table and chairs. Lowering the walking stick, he stepped into the darkened room and saw Maddie curled in a ball on the couch.

"What's wrong?" he said as he dropped his make-shift weapon.

"What are you doing down here, Quinn?" She turned to face him.

"I heard someone. When I didn't see a light, I was afraid you had an intruder." He should have checked her room, he realized. He'd let his fear take over.

She looked at the walking stick on the floor and her mouth curved up. "Thank you. I'm sorry I woke you. I thought I was being quiet."

"You were." His cop instincts always bubbled just below the surface. An unidentified sound still woke him from a deep sleep.

He lowered himself onto the other end of the couch. Her hair was a dark mass around her shoulders, and she wore the same shirt and plaid pajama pants. "Couldn't sleep?"

"No." She rested her chin on her knees. "I can't shut my mind off. I'm thinking too much."

"About what?" Him? That kiss?

"Everything." She traced one of the flowers on the couch upholstery, then finally looked at him. "J.D., for one. Why is he so angry?"

Quinn sighed. "His wife ran off with one of his friends. After the divorce, he started seeing Crystal Evans, your predecessor at the Harp. Then Crystal dumped him because he was still upset about his wife. He got a lot of sympathy, but he's been such a jerk lately that people are getting over it."

"Poor guy."

"That doesn't excuse him."

"I was stupid to step in front of him. Everyone in town is going to be laughing at me."

"Yeah, everyone will be talking about how you stood up to J.D." He smiled. "They might laugh, too. But at J.D.'s expense."

She stifled a yawn. "Jen told me that dumb-ass Gervano paid his bill at the Cherry Tree with a YourMarket credit card. Everyone in town is going to know we met."

"Don't worry about that tonight. Just go to sleep."

She leaned her head against the cushion. Her eyes were starting to droop. "Quinn? I'm glad you stayed."

"I didn't stay tonight because you're an employee."

"No?"

He rubbed his finger over her knuckles. "I have pretty

generous employee benefits, but sleepovers are definitely not part of the package."

"You mean you wouldn't stay with Andre?" Her eyes were closed and he could see the tension draining out of her muscles.

"Not Andre, not Jen, not another waitress. Only you, Maddie."

"That's good," she said, her voice soft in the darkness. Her hands slipped off her knees.

"Why?"

She smiled dreamily. "Because I want you for myself."

God. She must be talking in her sleep.

Moving slowly, his body painfully aroused, he slid her onto his lap. "Go ahead and sleep, sweetheart," he whispered. "You're safe with me."

Except she wasn't. Because he wanted her.

She snuggled into him, resting her cheek against his chest and wriggling her rear end into his groin. Clenching his teeth, he stroked her back and pushed her hair out of her face.

Faint freckles dotted her nose and cheeks. Her lips were parted, and he wanted to run his tongue over them and taste her again. One dark red curl lay over her nose, lifting with each breath she took. He tucked it behind her ear.

She shifted in his arms, brushing her breast against his hand. He had promised himself he wouldn't look below her neck, but he couldn't help himself.

Her T-shirt was white, the material thin and worn. The steady rise and fall of her chest pushed her nipples against it. Their dark shadows mesmerized him.

He hadn't wanted a woman this badly in a long time.

Maybe not ever. He tangled his fingers in her hair and pressed her head closer. The way he felt would be way too scary if she lived in Otter Tail. He'd back away so fast he'd leave skid marks on her porch.

But Maddie didn't live here. She was just staying for a while. Until she sold the Harp.

Then she'd leave, and he would be safe again.

# CHAPTER FOURTEEN

MADDIE SURFACED from sleep slowly. The sun pressed against her eyelids, and she turned her head to soak it up. It was as comforting as an embrace.

Her legs were warm, she realized drowsily. Warmer than the rest of her. She must have flung off her covers.

She opened her eyes and saw leaves fluttering on the maple tree on David's lawn. The tree outside the screened porch. She blinked, then remembered coming down here last night. She must have fallen asleep.

She tried to sit up and her feet pushed against a body.

Quinn. She'd been sleeping with her feet draped over his lap. He was slumped on the couch, his head against the cushion, his legs sprawled out in front of him. Asleep.

How had that happened? She remembered coming downstairs and curling up on the couch. She remembered Quinn finding her in the dark. She remembered him sitting down, vaguely recollected talking to him. But she had no memory of what they'd said.

She tried to slide her legs off his lap. Without opening his eyes, he put his arm across them, trapping them on his thighs. One of his hands slipped into the leg of her pajama bottoms and lazily caressed her calf.

Okay, then. He was awake, and she wasn't going to be able to pretend this hadn't happened. "Quinn?"

"Hmm." He pressed a finger against the back of her knee.

"You want to let go of my leg?"

"Not particularly."

She bent forward and brushed his hand away, then swung her legs off his lap. "Did you spend the night there?"

"Yeah." He sat up.

"You shouldn't have done that. You're going to be stiff," she said.

He opened his eyes and gave her a slow smile that made her heart flutter. "Promises, promises."

"You wish," she said, standing. Her muscles quivered as he watched her from half-open eyes. "I'll make coffee."

"Not yet." He caught her hand as she tried to walk past him. "Sit down and talk to me first."

"I don't talk to anyone before I have coffee," she said, disentangling her hand from his.

"That doesn't include me, does it?"

"*Especially* you."

She stepped into the kitchen and started a pot of coffee. Then, looking down at herself, she ran upstairs and threw on underwear, jeans and a different T-shirt. She was *not* having breakfast with Quinn in her pajamas, especially after last night. Finding herself practically sleeping in his lap was unnerving enough.

By the time she walked downstairs, he was standing in the kitchen with a coffee. He handed her a mug and she took a drink.

"Let's see your face," he said, setting his cup on the counter.

"It's fine." It looked horrible—an ugly mix of purple and red. "Just a little sore."

Ignoring her, he tilted her head to the side. His hands dropped away and curled into fists. "I'm going to beat the crap out of J.D."

"Let it go, Quinn. I don't want to bail you out of jail." Her body might still want him, but she knew better. She hoped.

After another sip of coffee, Quinn said, "You always this surly in the morning?"

"No. I'm trying to control myself because I have company. Usually I'm worse."

"Good to know," he said, letting his eyes drift over her. "Next time I won't take it personally."

Thank goodness she'd gotten dressed. Her nipples tightened beneath his gaze. "There isn't going to be a next time."

He raised an eyebrow. But instead of challenging her, he pulled a stool up to the kitchen island and sat. She was vaguely disappointed.

"Tell me about when you used to come to Otter Tail."

"What?" She set her coffee on the granite counter. "Where did that come from?"

"I spilled my guts last night. This morning it's your turn."

"Why do you think there's anything to tell?"

"We teased you when you were a kid," he said. "I'm guessing we were mean. You must have hated it."

"*You* didn't tease me."

"I was a self-absorbed little prick. I probably ignored you."

"Pretty much."

"You said David was your father's best friend."

He wasn't going to let this go. "They met in college. My father died when I was a baby, but David kept in touch with my mother. He was my godfather. When I was thirteen, he invited me to stay with him for the summer." She stared into her coffee, remembering how much she'd adored David. How much she hated everything else about Otter Tail.

"Your mother didn't mind you being gone for so long?"

Her mom had been thrilled to be rid of her. "She thought it was good for me to get out of the city."

"How many summers did you spend here?"

"Four."

He cocked his head. "So what did you do all summer?"

She smiled. "David had just bought this house. He was fixing it up, and he had a new project every year. I—" she mimed quotation marks "—helped him. I'm sure I was in the way, but he told me what a great job I was doing and how I made everything easier. I ate it up with a spoon."

"David didn't say things he didn't mean."

*Except about the Harp, apparently.* "I loved feeling useful and appreciated. He even got me my own set of tools. And I learned how to use them." Those tools had been so important to her. So much that she'd tried to emulate David in renovating houses, with disastrous results.

"You didn't hang around much with the other kids, did you?"

Her smile faded. "No. I was chubby and shy, and self-conscious the way only a teenage girl can be. I had acne and much brighter red hair than I do now. I was a freak."

"Considering how you look today, I highly doubt that."

"Thank you, but you wouldn't have noticed me back then." *Even when she'd asked him to.*

"My loss."

"No, it wasn't. I was a total goofball." She sighed. "Too bad you can't just skip your teenage years."

"You know an awful lot about Otter Tail kids for someone who didn't hang out with us."

She felt her face flame and sipped her coffee to hide it. "I used to watch you all…"

"Were we that interesting?"

She jumped up too quickly and the chair almost toppled over. He steadied it. "What's wrong?"

"Don't remind me how pathetic I was. I'd walk to town and see everyone in the Cherry Tree. Or hanging around in Mrs. Madsen's general store."

"What aren't you telling me, Maddie?"

He'd always been observant. Even that night at the beach. Maybe it was time to tell him what she'd done. To reveal the secret that had both shamed and thrilled her.

She walked over to the window and looked out at the lake. The beach at the bottom of the hill was barely visible, a sliver of golden sand against the blue water.

"I used to spy on the kids who used the beach below David's house," she said in a low voice. "They'd have parties there, drink beer, make out. I watched them from the woods."

He stood behind her but didn't touch her. "You wanted to join them."

"Desperately." But she'd been too afraid of rejection, so she'd hung back. Once, she'd heard one of the girls describe her as "that city girl who thinks she's better than everyone else," and Maddie had been shocked. She'd thought she wasn't good enough, that none of them would want to be friends with her.

"You should have. They were nice kids, for the most part. They would have welcomed you." He touched her shoulders, caressed her upper arms.

Okay, she had to finish this. She turned to face him. "I saw you once."

"Yeah? I used to drink beer there pretty regularly."

"You weren't drinking that night."

"What was I doing?"

She took a deep breath. "You were having sex. And you saw me watching you."

"What?" His hands tightened on her arms. "That was you? Watching me make out on the beach?"

She nodded.

She remembered him kissing the girl, and the moonlight had played over his naked body as they moved together. He must have felt Maddie watching, though, because he'd glanced up. She hadn't looked away. Neither had he.

She'd wished it had been her on the beach with Quinn. The idea had both shocked and aroused her.

The girl's low moans had gotten louder, then she'd cried out as she climaxed. Quinn had closed his eyes and groaned as he joined her, and Maddie had realized she was damp and aching. When Quinn collapsed onto the blanket, still entwined with the girl, Maddie had crept away.

The next week, she'd tried to seduce Quinn at the party. She hadn't cared if he was in love with that other girl. She'd wanted him that badly.

That was the last summer she'd spent in Otter Tail.

"I remember," he said in a low voice. "I was dating Amber Detweiler. I saw someone watching us, and…" He paused. "And it turned me on even more. I can't believe I'm saying this. I always wondered who that was."

"It was me. I knew it was wrong." But she hadn't stopped watching. She'd been both terrified and hopeful that he'd realize it was her.

"Is that why you didn't want to tell me who you were when you came back? You were afraid I'd recognize you?"

"It would have been completely mortifying." It still was. But she wanted him to know.

He traced a finger down her cheek. "Did you wish it had been *you* naked on the beach? Making love?" he asked, his voice raspy.

*Yes.* "I was only sixteen," she said, her voice breathy. "I'd never even had a boyfriend." Let alone sex. But she'd known exactly what they were doing. Wanted to be doing it herself. With Quinn.

"You're not sixteen anymore," he said. He watched her with half-closed eyes, his face taut with desire. "And I'm not a kid who's too horny to have any finesse."

"Amber Detweiler didn't look like she was complaining," Maddie said, stepping away from him. Away from temptation.

"I'd make sure you wouldn't have any complaints, either."

She was very sure she wouldn't. "Good to know," she said, putting more distance between them. "But I think I'll pass."

"Let me know if you change your mind." His eyes twinkled. "I hate to see you burdened by old memories."

"That's very generous of you, Quinn." She picked up her coffee and smiled easily. "But it's one of those memories that never go away. The things you remember from childhood that still make you squirm. You must have memories that still embarrass you."

He shrugged. "I pretty much did whatever I wanted when I was a kid. Didn't feel bad about any of it, either. At least not then. "

"I noticed," she said drily.

"I was a teenage boy, Maddie. A walking hormone. And I was angry at the world."

"How come?"

He rolled one shoulder. "My mom took off when I was eight. My dad didn't react well. He started to drink. It went downhill from there."

"Your mother left you?" Maddie's own mom was no great shakes in the parenting department, but at least she'd made some effort. And they'd managed to reconcile before she'd passed away a few years ago.

"She never wanted to be a mother," he said with a shrug. "She got pregnant way too young, had to get married. I cut into her partying in a big way."

"Poor Quinn."

"Don't feel sorry for me. I survived."

But not without scars. "Childhood should be about more than surviving."

"I'm not the only kid who had it rough." He studied her. "Sounds like you did, too."

"I did fine." She sipped at the coffee. "Especially now that I've confessed my deep, dark secret."

"Is that what it was? A confession?" His gaze was as intimate as a touch.

Her skin tingled with awareness. "Yes. I've always felt bad about it."

"We'll have to work on reframing your memories."

His words sent a ripple of longing and desire through her. "I don't think that's on the agenda for today."

His dimple flashed. "I'm devastated. I'll have to work on my presentation."

He wouldn't have to work very hard. The connection between them was growing stronger and stronger. More and more difficult to resist. Did he feel it, too?

Did it scare him as much as it scared her?

He finished his coffee and set the mug on the counter. "Want me to stick around? Try to change your mind?"

She did, and that was the wrong answer. "I'm sure you have more important things to do today," she said lightly.

"I have plans. Nothing more important, though."

She had to get out of this morass of desire and need churning through her. Had to back off, or she'd make a huge mistake. "I'm going to talk to Laura today," she blurted.

He froze, then picked up his empty mug and set it in the sink. "Did you get another offer for the Harp?"

"No. I just need to check in with her." Maddie wanted to touch him, to reassure him, but she didn't move. "I'd tell you if another offer came in."

"Would you give me a chance to make a counteroffer?"

"Of course. I don't want you to lose the Harp."

He looked around the kitchen. "What about this house? Are you selling it, too?"

"I was planning on it. But now that I'm here, I can't bear the thought. So, no. I'm not."

"If you sold it, you could take my offer for the Harp."

"I could. Either you get what you want, or I do."

"Tough choice, Maddie. Just remember, David wanted me to have the Harp."

"And he wanted me to have this house. Why should I give up what *I* want for you, Quinn? I like you." More than she should. "But this house is important to me."

"The Harp is important to *me.*"

Stalemate. "Thank you for staying with me last night," she said wearily. "I was glad you were here."

He nodded. "I'll see you this afternoon. We close at nine on Sunday nights, but your shift starts at four. Okay?"

"I'll be there." She watched until his truck disappeared from view, battling the need to call his cell phone and ask him to come back.

# CHAPTER FIFTEEN

QUINN GLANCED IN THE rearview mirror as David's house disappeared behind him.

Maddie's house now.

She didn't want to sell it. She'd made that clear.

He couldn't blame her. He loved that house. He wouldn't want to sell the old Victorian, either.

But if she didn't, he'd lose the Harp.

He slammed the steering wheel with his fist. He wasn't in control of his life any longer, and he didn't like it. He'd regained control the day he'd put the bottle of Jameson into the cupboard at the bar, and now it was all slipping away.

As he headed through town, he slowed down. He'd go nuts, staring at the walls of his house all day. So instead, he pulled into the parking lot at the pub. At least he could get some work done.

Once inside the dimly lit space, he stared at the dusty whiskey bottle, but he didn't take it down. He sat at the bar, opened his laptop and scrutinized his financial statements. He forgot about the bottle as he tried to figure out a way of pulling together more money.

The scrape of the door opening caught his attention. "Sorry," he called. "We're closed."

Andre stood in the doorway, the morning light shining behind him. "Quinn?"

What was Andre doing here? "Come on in," Quinn said, closing the laptop.

The cook wore a pair of jeans and an old tee with a beer logo on it, and running shoes that were scuffed at the toe. "What can I do for you?" Quinn asked.

"I heard you haven't found a cook and the kitchen's been closed," Andre said.

"And…?" Keeping his face impassive, Quinn watched the other man.

"You're losing money." Andre shifted his feet and relaxed a little.

"I have someone here part-time, and she'll be full-time in a week or two. We'll be fine until then."

"You found another cook?" Andre's expression tightened.

"You're not the only one in Door County who can put together a good meal, Andre." Quinn glanced at his watch. "Was there something you wanted?"

"Get rid of the waitress and I'll come back to work for you."

"Is that right?" Quinn straightened on the bar stool. "You're willing to make a deal with me?"

Andre shrugged. "Sure. No hard feelings."

"Yeah, there *are* hard feelings, Andre. You walked out on me and left customers waiting. Why would I want to take you back?"

"You're losing money and I can start tonight." He smirked. "People like my food. I know the kitchen. It's going to take a while for someone else to get up to speed."

Andre's cockiness had always irritated Quinn. He should have fired the guy a long time ago, but people *did* like his food. "Not good enough," he said. "You were a pain in the neck when you worked here."

Anger flared in the other man's eyes, but he quickly concealed it. "I need this job, Quinn. I have a family."

"I know you do, and I feel sorry for them, but you should have thought of that earlier."

"You're going to be sorry, man," Andre said, his expression darkening.

"Now you're threatening me? Get out of here, Andre. We're done talking."

The other man held his gaze for a long moment. "Watch your back, Murphy," he finally said. "And the waitress's, too."

The door slammed behind him, and Quinn strode to the door and watched Andre get into his car and drive off. When he'd disappeared, Quinn picked up the phone and dialed David's house. The phone rang five times, then voice mail picked up.

Why wasn't Maddie answering her phone? And why hadn't he bothered to get her cell phone number?

What if Andre was on his way to her house?

Quinn shoved the computer beneath his arm and ran out of the pub to his truck. Moments later, he was heading toward Maddie's.

MADDIE KNOCKED at the door of Delaney's workshop. Maybe she should have called before coming over to look at David's desk. The hard beat of a rock song pounded inside, and over that she heard the rumble of a machine.

Delaney wasn't going to hear her knock. Maddie cautiously opened the door and walked into the pole barn. The air inside was cool, and dust danced in the sunbeams pouring through the windows. The barn smelled of fresh wood, varnish and coffee. Delaney's drum set sat in one corner, and an assortment of tables, chairs, beds and chests were scattered haphazardly across the rest of the space. Polished oak, maple, cherry and walnut pieces glowed like satin.

A doorway at the other end of the room obviously led to Delaney's work area. The music was coming from a boom box on a table near the door. "Delaney?" she called.

"Back here." Her voice came over the whine of a saw.

As she walked toward the sound, Maddie ran her hand over the surface of a china cabinet she passed. She could picture it in David's dining room, full of David's Fiestaware. Pictured herself taking the dishes out, setting the dining room table.

As if David's house was her home. The place she belonged.

Her hand stilled on the smooth wood. No place had ever felt like that.

When she walked through the wide doorway, Delaney was stacking several pieces of wood on a worktable. The sharp tang of freshly cut lumber hung in the air. She lifted her safety glasses and turned off the music.

"Sorry," she said. "I play it loud so I can hear it while I'm working." Her gaze lingered on Maddie's cheek, where the bruise was still visible beneath her makeup. "Want some coffee?"

"I'd love some." She'd been too nervous with Quinn this morning to drink more than a few sips.

After she'd taken a gulp, she glanced at the large machines in the room. "Quite the collection."

"Just the usual," Delaney said with a shrug. "Lathe, joiner, table saw, jigsaw, planer, drill press, milling machine. Nothing like a good power tool to set a girl's heart to beating."

"A woman who considers power tools this big 'just the usual'?" Maddie raised her eyebrows. "I'm impressed."

"They're like any other tool. Drums, for instance. Once you learn how to use them, they're not intimidating anymore."

"Drums, maybe. That thing?" Maddie nodded at the table saw. "No way."

Delaney laughed. "We have to face our fears, Maddie. Want me to teach you?"

"No, thanks." She shuddered. "Although you must know what you're doing. Your furniture is beautiful. Works of art."

"Thanks." Her expression softened as she set down her coffee. "Let me show you David's desk."

Maddie followed her through the maze of finished furniture to a desk in the corner. Cherry. Her favorite wood.

A hutch sat on the desk, with a series of slots along the top. Beneath the slots were shelves, and the desk itself had drawers down both sides.

"It's gorgeous," Maddie exclaimed. "Exactly what I would have picked out for myself."

"David was really specific," Delaney said, brushing away an imaginary speck of dust. "He knew what he wanted." She shoved her hands into the pockets of her baggy jeans. "I was surprised he asked me to make it," she admitted. "He was already sick, and anxious for me to finish it."

David had had it built for her, Maddie realized. As she gazed at the beautiful piece, her eyes filled with tears. Every writer needed a workspace, he'd said, after she'd told him she wrote at the kitchen table on her laptop. They'd discussed what would make the perfect desk.

Then he'd had Delaney build it.

"You okay, Maddie?"

She sniffled. "It reminds me of David. Did he ever get to see it?"

"Before I stained and varnished it," Delaney answered. "He seemed pleased."

"Of course he was." A thought struck her. "Did you make the kitchen cabinets in his house, too?"

"I did." Delaney smiled again. "First ones I made. It took a while."

David had refinished the kitchen the way he thought Maddie would want it.

"I love them," she said in a low voice. He'd been preparing the house for her. Getting it ready for her to live there. How could she sell it now?

She couldn't. Not even to save Quinn's pub.

"I was kind of surprised when he renovated it," Delaney said. "There was nothing wrong with the old one. But it turned out great." She laughed. "Almost wonderful enough to make me want to take up cooking, but I lay down until the urge passed."

"I like to cook," Maddie said. She hadn't had much

of a chance yet, but she would put David's kitchen to good use.

"All this talk about cooking is making me itchy. Let's take a look at my calendar and figure out when I can deliver the desk for you."

As they headed back toward the workshop, a car door slammed. Moments later, Jen walked in, followed by two boys. The older one had shaggy blond hair, green eyes and glasses. He didn't look much like Jen, except for the blond hair. The younger boy had dark hair and dark eyes—and was the image of Tony Summers, Maddie remembered.

"Hi, Delaney," Jen said.

The younger boy rushed over, the older one trailing behind with studied adolescent boredom. "Hey, Delaney. We found instructions for making slingshots on the Web," the younger one said. "Can we use your wood scraps?"

"Of course," Delaney said. "You know which tools you can use."

The two boys headed into the other room, and Jen spotted Maddie.

"Hey, Maddie, what are you doing here?"

"David had this desk built before he…" She swallowed. "I came out to see it and arrange to have it delivered."

"How's your face?" She craned her neck to look at Maddie's cheek.

"It's fine." She touched the area, relieved that the pain was only a dull ache.

"What happened?" Delaney asked.

"J.D. punched her last night at the Harp," Jen related.

Delaney's mouth dropped open. "He what?"

"Not on purpose," Maddie said hastily. "He was trying to hit Quinn."

"My God." Delaney hoisted herself onto a table. "Spill. I want details."

Maddie explained what had happened, and Delaney whistled. "Glad *our* band wasn't on. Paul probably would have started playing the Rocky song. Just to get people riled up."

Maddie suppressed a laugh. She could see Paul doing just that. "Everyone was wonderful," she said. "Very solicitous. Augie Weigand offered to teach me to box."

"So what did Quinn do?" Delaney asked. "Close the bar so he could take you home?"

"Of course not," Maddie said, but her face got warm. "Sue Schmidt drove me home."

Jen crossed her arms and leaned against a table. "I bet he came over later to check on you," she said shrewdly.

"Of course he did. He felt responsible."

"And…?" Delaney asked.

"And what?" Maddie tried to look bewildered, but judging from Jen's grin, didn't succeed.

"He stayed, didn't he?" she pressed.

Maddie started to deny it, then sighed. "I couldn't get him out of the house." She held up her hands when Jen and Delaney exchanged knowing looks. "He slept in David's bedroom. Nothing happened."

"You wouldn't hold out on us, would you?" Jen asked. "We haven't had dates in so long we've forgotten what it's like to have a guy stay over. We need you to refresh our memories."

"Sorry, I need my memory refreshed, too."

"From what I could see the other night, Quinn looks like he's volunteering for the job," Delaney said.

And Maddie had been ready to take him up on the offer. "That would be really stupid, since he wants to buy the Harp from me."

"You're going to sell it to him, aren't you?" Delaney asked.

"I'd like to, but it's not that simple."

"Hey, Mom, we made slingshots." Jen's oldest son slouched out of the workshop, holding a vaguely Y-shaped toy made from varying sizes of wood scraps. "I know it's lame, but Tommy wants to go outside and try them."

"Come here, Nick." When the two ambled over, she introduced them to Maddie. "Go ahead, but stay on Delaney's property."

"Duh, Mom." Nick was already halfway out the door.

"Nice kids," Maddie said.

"Most of the time," Jen agreed. "Although Nick is into that teenaged 'everything about you is an embarrassment' stage. My parents are great and look after them a lot, but I need to spend more time with them."

She turned to Delaney. "I'm quitting the Cherry Tree. Finally." She nudged Maddie. "Thanks to her, for insisting Quinn let me cook at the Harp."

*Jen was quitting her job? What if the Harp had to close?* "So you're definitely going to cook for Quinn?"

"I start full time in two weeks," Jen said happily. "Martha said she'd need time to find another waitress. The first step in my master plan."

"What's your master plan?" Maddie asked.

"I want to open my own restaurant."

So if she sold the Harp to YourMarket, Maddie would be destroying Jen's dream, too. Should she tell her that Quinn might not buy the Harp? That it might not be there in a few months? "Um, what if Quinn doesn't buy the place? Would you be able to go back to the Cherry Tree?"

Jen's smile faded. "Are you really going to sell it to YourMarket?"

"They haven't even made an offer yet," Maddie said. "Who knows if they will? I'm just asking."

"YourMarket?" Delaney looked from Jen to Maddie. "You're going to sell the Harp to that company?"

"One of their reps called me. That's all."

"Do you have any idea how much traffic that store would bring into town?" Delaney demanded. "How many people would come through here?"

"More people might be good for the town," Maddie said. "It might help other businesses."

"Now you sound like Gordon Crawford." Delaney ran her hand through her short blonde hair, and Maddie saw a flicker of fear in her eyes. Why would Delaney be afraid of YourMarket?

"Hey, guys, take it easy. I haven't sold it to anyone yet. I'd *like* to sell it to Quinn, okay?"

There was an uncomfortable silence, then Jen said, "Maybe we should get those tables in my van before the boys destroy your garden." She turned to Maddie. "Delaney refinished a pair of end tables for my parents."

"Let me help," Maddie offered.

After a tiny pause, Delaney said, "Thanks. You can hold the doors open for us."

After the two end tables were loaded into the back of the van, Jen leaned against the door. "I was going to ask you if you wanted to go to Sturgeon Falls for dinner tonight," she told Delaney. "Maddie, do you want to come with us?"

She didn't want to make an awkward evening for Jen and Delaney. And right now, with the tension vibrating off Delaney, that's what it would be. "Thanks," she said. "I'd love to, but I have other plans. Maybe another time, okay?"

"Sure," Delaney said, not quite meeting her eyes. "We try to go out every couple of weeks."

"Ask me next time," Maddie said.

"Will do." Jen smiled. "We'll miss you tonight."

"Thanks." Maybe Jen would. Delaney? Not so much. "I'll call you to set up a delivery time," Maddie told her.

"Sure."

Maddie got into her car and pulled out of the driveway. Sunlight filtered through the maple trees, dappling the ground with gold, but she couldn't enjoy the scenery as she drove home.

The ripples in the pond from that one stone she'd dropped were spreading farther and farther. The pressure was ratcheting up, bit by bit.

It had all seemed so simple before she'd arrived in Otter Tail.

Sell the pub. Sell David's house. Pay Hollis back. Pay off the rest of her debts. Go home to Chicago and start over with a clean slate.

Now when she thought about home, it was David's

house. Ironic, since she'd spent her teenage years hating everything about Otter Tail.

How could home be the place she'd been running away from for the past fifteen years?

# CHAPTER SIXTEEN

"WHERE THE HELL have you been?" Quinn demanded as soon as she walked into the Harp that afternoon.

Maddie made a show of looking at her watch. "You said you opened at four on Sundays. Which means I'm early. So what are you talking about?"

"Earlier this afternoon. Where were you?"

She froze, shocked at his tone. "You want to rephrase that?" she finally asked as she grabbed her apron. "So you'd have a chance of getting an answer?"

He closed his eyes and took a breath. "I drove to the house about an hour after I left you there. I was worried."

"I had some business with Delaney Spencer," she said. "I wasn't gone very long. I must have just missed you." She tilted her head. "Why did you need to see me? What's wrong?"

A muscle in his jaw twitched. "Andre came in this morning. Asking for his job back. It got ugly when I turned him down."

"Did he threaten you?"

"I'm not worried about myself. Andre isn't going to mess with me."

"You think he'll come after me?" Astounded, she stared at him. "Why would he do that?"

"I really doubt he'll do anything. But he was angry and made a couple of threats."

"Did you call the police?"

"Yeah, I talked to Brady Morgan. He's going to keep an eye on your place and mine. And the Harp."

"That's crazy." She remembered vividly the cook's anger when he'd stormed out of the Harp, but she shrugged to hide her uneasiness. "Andre strikes me as the type who's all talk and no action."

"And you'd know this, how?"

"I live in Chicago, Quinn. I work with contractors, electricians and plumbers. I can handle a cook."

"Yeah, you're tough." His expression softened. "Tough enough to take a punch for me last night."

"I wasn't exactly planning on letting him make contact."

"But you did, and I couldn't stop J.D. Just like I can't control Andre."

She paused in the act of tying her apron. She should have figured it out. He was upset because he couldn't protect her. "You must have been frantic when you couldn't find me earlier."

"Yeah."

"You're going to make me think you care," she said lightly, although her heart began to race. Quinn had been more than worried. He'd been furious. Terrified. For her.

"Of course I care." He grabbed a rag and wiped it over the bar. So he didn't have to look at her? "You're working here, so I'm responsible for you."

The warm fuzzies disappeared faster than an ice cube

on a hot stove. "Don't worry," she said as she knotted the apron strings with a yank. "I'm not going to sue you."

She tugged at the apron to straighten it before she started serving the early arrivals. But she felt his gaze following her as the afternoon became evening.

Finally, when they had a momentary lull, he asked, "What's with the new work outfit?"

So they were going to ignore the whole topic of Andre, and Quinn's reaction. Fine. She smoothed down her flirty denim skirt. She'd worn it because the only pair of jeans she'd brought with her had split at the knee. "Change of pace," she said. "Is it a problem?"

"Not at all." His gaze lingered on her legs. "I like it. A lot."

Apparently the customers liked it, too. Her tips were better, but she had to fend off more hands than usual. She was going to have to use some of her carefully hoarded cash to buy another pair of jeans tomorrow. "Don't get used to it. It's a one-night-only deal."

"Is that right?" He lifted his smoldering eyes to hers. "Then I better enjoy it while I can."

Her pulse leaped and she couldn't look away. She told herself they had major issues to deal with, but it didn't seem to make any difference. The sounds of the pub receded until she heard only the pounding of her own pulse, felt only her flushed face.

"How about another beer, Maddie?" Steve Gladwin stepped in front of her, waving his glass, and the spell was broken.

"Sure, Steve," she said, noting that the man was swaying a little on his feet. "Where are you sitting?"

He waved toward the back of the pub, and she saw his two buddies in a booth. "Let's get you back to your friends."

She led him through the crowd, and when she reached the table, she saw that one of the men was drinking soda. "You're driving?" she asked Ray Nolan quietly.

"Yep."

Maddie nodded. "Anyone else need a refill?"

The third man lifted his glass, and Maddie guided Steve into the booth. "I'll be right back, guys."

As she walked away, she saw Frank Gervano leaning against the bar, drinking whiskey. He raised his glass to her when he caught her staring. In dread, she forced herself to ignore the YourMarket representative.

"We heard what happened last night with J.D.," Steve said, enunciating each word carefully as she set their beers on the table. "Shall we escort you home tonight?"

"Thanks, Steve," Maddie said, smiling. "That's very sweet of you. But I'll be okay. It was an accident."

"J.D.'s wife messed with his head," Steve answered. He nodded like a bobblehead doll. "But that's no excuse for what he did. We'll straighten him out if he comes in here again. Right, guys?"

The other two men murmured in agreement. Ray said, "I'll be happy to give you a ride home if you need it, Maddie. All you have to do is ask."

"I appreciate that," she replied, feeling touched.

Was she one of their own?

Or was she just a fool, desperate for the sense of community and kindness these men were showing her?

Maddie hurried away, unable to face Ray. He certainly wouldn't be kind if she sold the Harp to YourMarket.

Throughout the evening, more than a few of the people she served made a point of asking her how she was doing, and assured her they hardly noticed the bruise. Paul Black told her Gordon Crawford wanted to build condos in Otter Tail and said they were looking for someone to run against him in the upcoming election.

"You interested?" he asked.

"I think a person should probably live here for more than five minutes before running for mayor." She glanced at Quinn, who was talking to Patrick O'Connor at the bar. "Have you asked Quinn?"

"He's not interested in getting involved."

*In anything.* "Too bad," she said lightly. "I think he'd be good for the town."

"Yeah, so do I." Paul shrugged. "Can't hold a gun to his head, though."

"What about you?" Maddie asked.

He laughed. "I can't be mayor. Everyone knows I oppose all forms of government."

"That's right. You're the big bad radical, aren't you?" She took his empty glass. "Want another one?"

"Make it a black-and-tan," he said, nodding toward the bar. "Quinn's got a stick up his butt, and it always irritates him when I order one of those."

"You're a troublemaker, Paul," she said, laughing.

"That's me." He smiled easily, but she thought she saw a shadow in his eyes.

AT THE END OF THE NIGHT, as Quinn was counting the money in the cash register, he said, "I'm taking you home."

"Why?" She paused in washing a table.

He stuffed the cash into a bank bag. "I spent the afternoon imagining all the horrible things that might have happened to you. I'm going to make sure you get into your house safely."

"I get it, Quinn. You were a cop and you've seen too much. But I'll be okay. Andre was just blowing smoke because he was angry."

"Probably," Quinn admitted. "But I won't be able to sleep tonight if I don't. So humor me, okay?"

*Stop with the mental pictures of Quinn in bed.* "Fine. Guilt works. You've already lost too much sleep because of me."

"You have no idea."

His voice was so low that she wondered if he'd meant her to hear. He grabbed another sponge and helped her wash the last few tables. It only took a few minutes to finish the last of the work, then Quinn turned out the lights. When they stepped into the pool of darkness at the side of the building, he took her hand.

"You think Andre is going to jump out at us like a killer in a horror movie?"

"Nah," he said, a grin in his voice. "I just like touching you."

*Okay, then.* Way to leave her speechless.

He waited while she got into her car, then climbed into his truck.

His headlights in her rearview mirror made her very aware of his presence. When she pulled into the driveway, the house was enveloped in darkness, and she slowed the car.

Quinn's truck door slammed and he opened her door. "What's wrong?"

"I left the porch lights on."

His mouth thinned. "Give me your house keys and stay in the car while I check it out."

She handed him the keys, then got out and followed him to the porch.

"Maddie, get in the car," he said, studying the house.

"I'm not going to cower while you play the hero."

He stared at her for a long moment and she stared right back. Finally, he sighed. "Stay behind me."

As they walked up the stairs to her front door, she heard the sound of a vehicle starting. It seemed as if it came from the road just beyond the trees at the back of the house. Quinn froze, then ran down the stairs and into the woods.

A few minutes later he returned. "All I saw were tail-lights. Too far away to tell anything about the car."

The porch lights had been smashed, and someone had spray-painted the word *bitch* on the floorboards. Quinn fumbled with the little penlight on Maddie's key chain and aimed it at the front door. He inserted the key and opened the lock.

"It doesn't look like he tried to get into the house," Quinn said.

He walked inside and switched on the lights. She followed him in, but stayed in the hall as he searched all the rooms on the first floor, then headed upstairs. Next he went into the basement. Finally he returned to the front hall.

"No sign of any disturbances," he said. "I checked the back door, too. Apparently, whoever it was just wanted to harass you." He slung an arm over her shoulders. "Come on into the kitchen and have a glass of wine."

He watched her out of the corner of his eye as if he expected her to refuse. She almost did.

But he'd told her that this was his problem, not hers. That he was fine with people drinking in front of him. If he wasn't here, she'd have a glass of wine.

"That sounds good," she said.

He smiled as he opened the bottle of wine that was on the counter, and poured her a glass. "Was that so hard?"

"It was. But I believe you when you tell me it's okay. You told me you wouldn't lie to me." The dark wine caught the light and gleamed red. She took a sip, glancing at him over the rim of the glass.

"Thank you," he said. His expression softened as he watched her take a drink. "One of the things I promised myself when I stopped drinking was that I wouldn't lie to anyone. I'd done too much lying to cover up my problem."

"Was it hard? Quitting?"

"It was hell," he said. "I was very fond of my Jameson." His mouth quirked into a smile. "Still am."

"Your family must be proud of you."

"I don't have any family left. My dad died years ago. From drinking." His gaze touched on all the pieces of David in the kitchen—the Fiestaware, the glass-fronted cabinets, the rich glow of cherry wood, the bottles of wine he'd left in the wine rack. "David was the closest thing I had to family."

"I adored him. He always made me feel good about myself."

"That was David." He smiled briefly. "I wouldn't have stopped drinking if it hadn't been for him."

"I'm not surprised," she said.

"It took him a while, but he convinced me I was killing myself. He said Donyell wouldn't have wanted me to die, too. And no woman was worth it."

"A woman?" Maddie sighed as she set the glass down on the table. With a man like Quinn, there was always a woman.

He stared out the darkened window. "She was a reporter. Television news. She dumped me when I quit. Apparently, she'd been going through my paperwork, looking for inside information on the cases I was working. But I was thinking with parts other than my brain."

"And that made the drinking worse." Maddie reached for his hand, and he twined his fingers with hers.

"Yeah. But it wasn't Jodie's fault. I'd been drinking since I was fourteen. I'd use any excuse to crack open a bottle."

"It still feels wrong to drink in front of you."

"You'll get used to it." He tapped a nail against the glass. "It would be a problem if you couldn't drink in front of me. You'd be resentful, I'd feel guilty and it would get ugly."

That implied they would be involved. Lovers. Her heart skipped a beat. Was that what she wanted?

*Yes.* To make love with him.

She squeezed his hand, let go and wandered onto the screened porch. The golden edge of a full moon was creeping over the horizon. She turned to Quinn impulsively. "Let's go down to the beach and watch the moon rise."

"All right." He opened the hall closet and pulled a blanket from the shelf. "It's chilly on the lake."

They locked the door behind them, then walked across the dew-moist grass toward the path. The light from the moon illuminated the steps on the wooden staircase and threw the foliage next to it deeper into shadow. A cocoon of moonlight surrounded them as they descended.

Quinn stopped a few steps up from the sand and pulled her down next to him. He wrapped the blanket around them, then draped his arm around her shoulder.

The wind sighed gently through the trees and tiny waves broke on the beach, spreading white foam over the dark sand, one after another. Moonlight glinted on the dark water, and every now and then she heard the splash of a fish.

His scent drifted over her, woodsy and alluring, and her heart thumped against her chest. He shifted on the stair and his leg bumped hers. The rough slide of denim over her bare skin made her catch her breath. He rolled his shoulders, and his fingers settled on her collarbone. Tiny sparks traveled straight to her heart.

She glanced at him out of the corner of her eye, but he appeared absorbed by the vista in front of them. She wriggled restlessly on the stair, and he pressed his thigh to hers.

"Whoever sprayed your porch tonight isn't hiding in the woods," he said. "We heard him drive away."

"I wasn't thinking about that." Right now, it was the furthest thing from her mind.

She wanted to feel the rasp of his five o'clock shadow against her lips. She wanted to taste the spot on his neck where his pulse beat steadily.

She wanted to crawl into his arms and stay there for a long, long time.

"You thinking about work?"

"Nope."

"About what to do with David's house?"

"Nope."

"About what to do with the Harp?"

"Not even that."

He shifted on the stair so he could look at her face, but didn't let her go. "Then by the process of elimination, you must be thinking about this." He brushed his lips over hers, and she shuddered. He smiled against her mouth. "Bingo."

He picked her up and settled her on his lap. "Maybe we should stay away from each other." He traced the shell of her ear with his tongue. "But that's not going to happen, Maddie. There's no way I can stay away from you."

He wanted her as much as she wanted him. Her heart stuttered and she found his mouth for a hot, urgent kiss. As she caressed his tongue with hers, his hands fumbled with the buttons of her blouse. The blanket he'd put over their shoulders fell away, and cool air blew over her chest. Moments later, he'd opened her bra and drawn the straps down her arms.

He broke their kiss, and she lifted her heavy eyelids.

He was leaning back, looking at her, the moonlight turning her skin milky-white. He cupped her breasts in his hands.

"God, I love your breasts," he murmured, placing small, sucking kisses along the curves. "They're perfect."

He rubbed his thumbs over her nipples once, then again, and she arched mindlessly. All that mattered was the way he made her body vibrate, the drumbeat that pounded through her, the need to have him inside her.

She reached for the bottom of his polo shirt and pulled at it, impatient to get her hands on him. He yanked it off and she ran her palms over his chest, feeling the iron-hard muscles beneath his hot skin, running her fingers over the coarse dark hair that arrowed down beneath the waistband of his pants.

When she fumbled for his belt, he stopped her. "Not yet," he murmured, sucking on her earlobe. His erection was hard beneath her, and she squirmed against him, desperate.

"You don't take orders well, do you?" he whispered into her ear before he sucked on her neck.

"Never have." She gasped when he burrowed beneath her skirt and trailed a hand up the inside of her thigh. "I prefer to give orders."

She felt him smile. "You can give me all the orders you want."

"Take off your pants," she said, kissing him again.

His chuckle vibrated against her. "In a minute."

"You're disobeying?" She caught her breath as his hand drifted higher. "You'll have to be punished."

"Now I'm scared." He caressed her bare ass, then

stilled. "A thong?" His fingers followed the tiny strip of material. "Did I mention that I love this skirt?"

"Is that right?" She rubbed her cheek against his chest, breathing in the cologne he wore. "Next time, I won't wear any underwear."

He sucked in a breath. "You're going to kill me, Maddie." He slipped his hand beneath the lacy thong, and she arched helplessly against him. He took the tip of one breast in his mouth as he stroked her slick crease. Her tension wound tighter and tighter.

"No," she panted. "Not alone."

"Yes," he whispered. "My turn to give orders. I want to watch you."

He increased the pressure as he swirled his tongue around her nipple, and she exploded, crying his name.

The waves of release went on and on until she lay in his arms, trembling and unable to move. He caressed her, feathering kisses across her face, murmuring endearments.

Finally she opened her eyes. "Why did you do that? I wanted you inside me when I came."

He smiled, nuzzling her neck. "We're just getting started."

# CHAPTER SEVENTEEN

QUINN SKIMMED HIS HANDS over her hips and up her sides. "You are so sexy," he murmured, nuzzling the shadowed valley between her breasts. "I can't stop touching you."

She shivered, and he picked up the blanket and drew it around her. "Come to the beach," he said.

His phone buzzed as he stood, but he ignored it. Taking her hand, he led her down the rest of the stairs onto the cool sand. He spread the blanket and she dropped onto it, her legs still wobbly. He stripped off his shoes and socks, took foil packets out of his pocket and yanked off his jeans. He stood naked in front of her, bathed in moonlight. "Come here," she whispered, holding out her hand.

The wind off the lake was cool on her hot, sweaty body, but she barely felt it. Dropping beside her on the blanket, Quinn gathered her close. "Cold?" he murmured.

"Mmmm," she said, smiling into his shoulder, feeling his ragged heartbeat beneath her fingers. "I know how you can warm me up."

"Yeah? Want to tell me?"

"I'd rather show you."

"I like the sound of that." He skimmed his hand down her arm, down her hip, down her leg. "As much as I love this skirt, it has to go."

He eased the zipper open, then slid the short denim garment down her legs. He hesitated at the thong. "Shame to get rid of this. Promise to wear it again?"

"I promise." She nestled closer to him, inhaling the scent of his skin, along with the smell of wood smoke.

"Someone must be having a campfire farther down the beach," she murmured, looking over his shoulder.

He glanced at the deserted expanse of sand on either side of them. "Not anywhere close. No one can see us." He nuzzled her neck. "Or were you hoping they could?"

"I've never made love in public. Where someone could watch me." She dragged her hands down his back and cupped his firm hips. His muscles flexed beneath her fingers.

"Really? I thought you were pretty adventurous." He eased one leg over hers. "Maybe there's someone in the woods spying on us," he whispered, brushing his mouth over hers. "Do you want me to stop?"

The thought of someone watching them, just as she had watched Quinn, made her heart race.

"No," she whispered, pulling him closer. "I love what you're doing to me."

"What if they see me doing this?" He swirled his tongue around her nipple.

"It doesn't matter. Don't stop," she gasped, arching into his mouth.

"How about this?" He reached down and cupped her.

"Quinn," she moaned. "Please. You're making me crazy. I don't care who's up there."

"Seeing you back then made me crazy," he said, kissing his way up her chest, her neck, to the corner of her mouth. "Now I don't want to share."

"Do *you* want to stop?" She wriggled against him. "In case someone's watching."

"I don't think I could." He trailed his mouth down to her navel as he opened one of the foil packets. "I want you too much."

He tensed for a split second, as if realizing what he'd just said. Then he kissed her again. "Let them watch," he said as he slid inside her.

For a moment he stayed perfectly still, watching her, his eyes heavy-lidded and his face taut with passion. He cupped her face in both hands, and she felt him trembling.

Then he began to move and she felt the tension building again, coiling more and more tightly. Holding his gaze, she held on to his hips and rose to meet him, matching his thrusts with her own. Her heart thundered, its beat matching his.

"Quinn," she cried as her climax swept over her.

He thrust again, then shuddered in her arms. When he kissed her neck, she thought she heard him whisper, "Maddie."

HOME, HE THOUGHT HAZILY, breathing in Maddie's scent, his body absorbing the slide of her skin over his, the feel of her arms and legs gripping him. He was home.

As their skin cooled, Quinn pushed the thought out of his mind. To distract himself, he trailed his fingers down her side. "You make me wild, Maddie." Since the first time he'd touched her. Hell, if he was honest, since the first time he'd seen her.

"No more than you make me. I can't believe we just had sex in a public place."

"What were we thinking?" He nuzzled her neck.

"The same thing we're going to be thinking in another few minutes if you keep that up."

"Did you like knowing we might have an audience?"

"I liked being the one with you instead of the one watching." Her breath tickled his chest, and he felt her lips curve as she kissed him.

"Me, too. I don't care if the whole world is watching. I don't care about—"

Warning bells clanged in his mind.

"Can we stay here forever, Quinn?" Her voice was dreamy and her muscles lax. "Just like this?"

Forever? He hadn't signed up for that. "You'd get cold," he said abruptly. He stood and tugged on her arm. "Come on, Sleeping Beauty. Let's go back to the house." He shook the sand out of the blanket, draped it around her shoulders, then steered her toward the stairs.

She wrapped her arm around his waist and snuggled, smiling, into him. They'd made love twice.

The cell phone in his pocket chirped again. *Saved by the voice mail.* When they got into the house, he tossed their clothes on a kitchen chair and flipped open his phone. He had ten missed calls.

"Let's go to bed," Maddie said, twining her arms around him from behind. Her breasts pressed into his back and her hands trailed over his abdomen.

"Hold on," he said, grabbing her wrist as he stared at the phone. He listened to the first voice mail and turned to stone.

Quinn dropped the phone on the kitchen table. "I have to go," he said, grabbing his pants. "The Harp is on fire."

Maddie stumbled backward. "What?"

"The fire chief has been trying to get hold of me," he said grimly, struggling to get his arms into his shirt.

"Oh, no!" She grabbed her own clothes and threw them on, hopping on one foot as she tried to jam her shoe onto the other.

"Stay here. I can deal with this."

"I'm sure you can, but I'm coming with you. If you don't want me in your truck, I'll drive myself."

He *did* want her with him, he realized uneasily. And he'd wanted to stay all night. "There's nothing you can do."

"You don't know that." She reached for her car keys. "I'll be right behind you."

"Fine. Let's go," he said impatiently. "We're wasting time."

She headed for the front door and he ran after her. Moments later they were in his truck, barreling down the short stretch of highway to town.

A cloud of smoke trailed lazily into the air above Otter Tail, but he didn't see any flames. The fire must be under control.

He slowed as he got closer. Three fire trucks sat in front of the Harp and a tangle of beige hoses snaked over the ground. A handful of gawkers stood in small clusters, kept well back from the fire engines by Cal Hodges, the police chief.

Parking the truck at a haphazard angle, Quinn jumped out and stared at the scene. Maddie grabbed his hand a second later.

Several windows were shattered. Scorch marks ran up the outside walls, and smoke drifted out of holes in the roof. All he could see through the broken glass was a mass of charred wood and smoke.

"The walls are still standing," Maddie murmured. "Maybe it's not as bad as it looks."

He'd seen plenty of fire scenes during his years as a cop. This was not good.

The fire chief saw him and stepped carefully over the hoses. "Where the hell were you, Quinn? I've been trying to get hold of you for over an hour."

"I didn't have my cell phone with me," he said. He'd been making love to Maddie while his pub burned down. "What happened?"

Don Taylor's mouth tightened. "Arson. We'll have to wait until the place cools down to confirm it, but it was classic. Multiple points of origin, and it got out of control way too fast. Someone driving by spotted it early and called it in, or everything would have been incinerated. As it is, I'm not sure how much of the place is salvageable."

"Was anyone hurt?"

"Nope. The fire department put it out pretty fast."

Maddie moved closer and Quinn let himself lean on her for a moment as he watched the smoke swirl around the ruined building. His place. He'd finally found where he belonged and what he wanted to do. Now it was gone.

"I'm sorry, Quinn," she murmured. "But you can rebuild it. You needed a bigger place, anyway."

"So the fire was a good thing?" He swung around to face her. "It makes everything easier, doesn't it?"

"Of course not." She cupped his face in her hands. "This is awful, but no one was injured. It's just a building, Quinn. You can build another one."

"But not on this land, right?"

She dropped her hands. "I didn't say that."

"This was a good resolution to your dilemma, wasn't it?"

"That hadn't even occurred to me," she said. "Believe it or not, I was more concerned about *you* than my 'dilemma.' I know you're upset. So am I. But—"

He saw Frank Gervano talking to Gordon Crawford, and anger ripped through him. He moved away from Maddie so abruptly that she stumbled.

"Is this what you were talking about, Gervano?" he demanded as he strode toward the two men. "Is this what you meant when you said properties can lose their value quickly? The Harp lost its value pretty damn fast tonight, didn't it?"

"What are you talking about, Murphy?"

Even dressed in jeans and a chambray shirt, the guy looked oily. "I'm asking if you burned down the Harp."

Gervano recoiled. "Of course I didn't."

Quinn looked at the man's hands. "I didn't mean you did it yourself," he said scornfully. "You might ruin that perfect manicure. So how did you work it? Who did you hire? That's how your company operates, isn't it? You don't let anything get in your way."

"Quinn, I know you're upset," Gordon Crawford said, stepping between the two men. "But that's no reason to accuse Frank of burning down your pub."

"Get away from me, Crawford," Quinn said, shoving the mayor. "Hell, maybe *you* did it. So you can *develop* the land." It felt as though they'd used a dull spoon to scoop his heart out of his chest. "How did you find out about this pub, anyway, Gervano? Laura Taylor sure as hell didn't contact you."

He caught a flicker of guilt in the mayor's eyes. "Damn you, Crawford." He grabbed the older man's shirt with one hand, curled the other into a fist. "Who gave you the right to mess with people's lives?"

"That's enough, Quinn." The police chief, Cal Hodges, caught Quinn's arm, then moved him out of reach of Gordon. "We don't know who's responsible. Beating people up isn't going to get us any answers." But he glared at Gordon and Gervano. "Could be other people with reason to burn the place down."

"Is that right, Cal? Who do you like for it?"

"I don't make assumptions," he said, holding Quinn's gaze. "Don's getting the fire inspectors in from Sturgeon Falls tomorrow, and we'll see what they have to say. "

Quinn watched Cal talk to Gervano and the mayor, anger churning. Don Taylor pulled him farther away from the men. "You going to settle down, son?" he asked quietly.

Quinn shook him off. His arms felt as if they were weighted down and his legs trembled as though they would give out any moment. "Get out of here, Don. Go do your job. Save what's left of my place."

The fire chief hesitated, then nodded once and walked away.

Quinn turned to Gervano and Crawford. "If either of you is responsible for this, you won't be able to run far enough or fast enough. I will destroy you. And I'm not stupid enough to do it in front of witnesses."

"Quinn, don't be ridiculous," Crawford blustered. "Of course we're—"

He stepped closer and the mayor stumbled back. "You never did know when to keep your mouth shut, Gordon," Quinn said in a low voice. "Get out of here. Now."

Crawford turned and hurried away. Gervano stared at Quinn for a beat, then followed.

Maddie approached him, holding out her hand. He wanted to take it and hold on tight. He wanted to lose himself in the depths of her green eyes, to wrap himself in the understanding he saw there.

He yearned for her, for her strength, for the comfort she offered.

And that scared the crap out of him. He didn't need Maddie.

He didn't need anyone.

"This is your fault," he said to her. "You brought Your-Market to Otter Tail, and they burned down my pub."

She dropped her hand. "What?"

"Your fault," he repeated. He heard his voice rise, but couldn't stop himself. "You want to sell my pub to them."

"You're upset. I understand." She clenched and unclenched her fists. "But I didn't contact YourMarket and I didn't burn down the Harp."

"You might as well have. If you hadn't been so

greedy, they wouldn't have gotten involved. You brought this ugliness."

"Stop before you say something you'll regret," Maddie said. "This is awful, but we'll figure out a way to fix it."

"*We'll* figure out a way? There is no *we*." He shoved his hands through his hair. "God, how could I have slept with you? What was I thinking?"

She flinched. "I don't know. You tell me."

The pain on her face was like a punch to his gut, but he couldn't stop himself. "You don't care about this town or anyone in it. Hell, you haven't even been here for fifteen years."

THE WHOLE SCENE—flashing lights of the fire trucks, the smoke from the Harp, the glare of streetlights—seemed to break into a million glittering pieces. Maddie felt her heart shrinking, getting smaller. Harder. Until she couldn't feel anything. "You want to know why I never came back to Otter Tail?" She drew a shuddering breath. "Remember what I told you about the beach…?" She swallowed and clenched her hands again. She'd told him far too much.

"Right after that night, there was a party. I'd never been to one of the parties before, but I went, hoping you might be there. You were."

Everything she'd felt that night came rushing back. The excitement. Her happiness at being included. Her anticipation of seeing Quinn. And the humiliation and embarrassment that had overwhelmed her as she'd fled.

"I made a pass at you. Clumsy and awkward. Stupid,

too, because I knew you had a girlfriend. You laughed. Asked why I thought you'd want to kiss me. A couple of the other kids laughed, too. Someone asked if the fat girl had a chance with Mad Dog." She'd heard that voice in her head for years. "I left Otter Tail a few days later and never came back."

"What are you talking about?" Some of the anger faded from his expression.

"I should have learned my lesson. I should never have gone near you this time. But I let you fool me. I let myself think you cared about me. It was all a game, wasn't it?" She swallowed. "You wanted the pub, and you thought the best way to get it was to screw it out of me. Or was that a pity screw after my little confession about watching you on the beach?"

He recoiled. "Maddie, I—"

She didn't let him finish. She couldn't bear to hear any more. "Thank God you opened my eyes. But you know what? You don't get to reject me again, Quinn. I'm rejecting you."

She turned and walked away, aware of his gaze on her back. Aware of the silence from the people around them.

David had always told her she had to control her impulsiveness, or it would get her into trouble. He'd been right.

She'd been right when she left town, too. There was a reason she'd stayed away for fifteen years.

## CHAPTER EIGHTEEN

THE CROWD GATHERED behind him went completely silent as Quinn watched Maddie walk away. He swung around and glared at them, and they shuffled their feet and murmured to one another. No one looked at him.

What the hell was the matter with Maddie? He couldn't remember what had happened at some stupid party fifteen years ago.

Just before she turned the corner, she stumbled over a bump in the sidewalk where a tree root had buckled the cement. Augie Weigand reached out to steady her as her sandal came off. Instead of putting it back on, she nodded at Augie, scooped up the shoe and kept walking.

Making Quinn feel like a piece of crap.

One of the fire trucks beeped as it backed up. For the first time, he had an unobstructed view of the ruins of the Harp. He sucked in a breath, blindsided.

*Maddie would have wrapped her arms around him.*

He remembered her hands cupping his face, her legs wrapped tight around his waist. How she'd clung to him as if she'd never let go.

What was wrong with him? He'd thought he had better control of his temper than that.

She'd scared him on a gut-deep level. So he'd done what he did with everyone. He'd pushed her away.

No wonder no one would look at him. No wonder they were all keeping their distance.

What happened to the Harp wasn't Maddie's fault. She'd just been the most convenient target. And he'd known exactly how to hurt her.

She needed to sell the place. But instead of complaining, she'd tried to comfort him.

Quinn slumped against the bumper of his truck. He should find her. Apologize. Make it right, somehow.

But ten minutes later, after wandering through town, he hadn't found her. Just like smoke rising from the ruins of the Harp, she'd vanished.

Maybe it was better that she had. He wiped his hands over his face, then stared at the soot smeared on his palms. Maybe it was better that it was over now. He'd only end up hurting her more in the long run.

He'd quit on Otter Tail when he'd left as a teen. Then he'd quit the police force. Now he'd quit on Maddie, less than an hour after they'd made love.

If she was smart, she'd want nothing more to do with him.

If *he* was smart, he'd stay as far away from her as possible.

He climbed into his truck and stared at the ruins of his pub. By the time the sun started to rise, only a few wisps of smoke drifted up from the blackened shell. The last of the firefighters had packed up and driven away, and the crowd had dispersed long ago.

He was alone.

MADDIE WOKE SLOWLY and resisted the urge to open her eyes. Something hovered on the edge of her consciousness, something dark. Something she didn't want to face.

*Quinn.*

She rolled over and stared at the canopy above her bed that Quinn said looked like an explosion in a ruffle factory.

She didn't want to think about him.

She couldn't think of anything else.

Finally, throwing off the covers, she padded downstairs to the kitchen. She needed coffee.

Pouring water into the coffeemaker, she told herself she should have had the Green Bay newspaper delivered. It would have given her something to do this morning. Something to focus on besides what had happened last night.

Who was she kidding? Nothing could push Quinn out of her head. They'd made love. More than once. It had been perfect. She'd felt as if she'd found the place she'd been searching for. In Quinn's arms.

An hour later, he'd told her he wanted nothing more to do with her.

Then she'd made a fool of herself in front of half the town.

She had to get out of here. How could she stay, now that Quinn had dumped her so publicly? After she'd revealed what had happened after the party. Next time she went to work, they would all know the truth.

*No.* There wouldn't *be* a next time at work. The Harp was gone. Nothing but ashes.

She'd go back to Chicago. Maybe it didn't feel like home anymore, but it was safe. She knew who she was in the Windy City. She hadn't built up any illusions about herself there.

Holding her coffee mug tightly in one hand, she found a pen and a pad of paper and began to write down what she'd need to do before she could leave. After "packing" and "call Laura," she faltered. The desk. David's desk. She'd have to arrange for Delaney to deliver it.

The desk belonged in David's house. Maddie had already picked a spot for it, next to a window in a nook in the library. She'd imagined watching the seasons change, putting out a couple of bird feeders. A slice of Lake Michigan was visible in the distance behind the trees. She'd been looking forward to seeing it gray and stormy in the fall, crusted with ice in the winter, bright blue in spring.

Opening her cell phone, she pressed Delaney's number. "Hi. It's Maddie," she said, when Delaney answered.

"How are you doing?" the other woman asked. "I heard about the Harp."

About her fight with Quinn, as well? "I'm okay," Maddie said wearily. "No one was hurt." *Except me.*

"Quinn must be pretty upset."

*Talk about an understatement.* "Yeah, he is. Listen, I forgot to set up a time for you to deliver the desk. When would work for you?"

Silence hung heavily for a moment. "What happened?" Delaney finally asked.

"Besides the Harp burning down? Isn't that enough?"

"Yeah, that's why I know something happened. Otherwise, you wouldn't be worrying about the desk."

Maddie pressed her fingers to the glass and stared

blindly at the lake. "I'll be busy trying to deal with the Harp, so I'm trying to get other things settled." Not exactly the truth, but not a lie, either.

Another silence. "Okay, Maddie. When do you want it?" Delaney's voice had cooled, and Maddie realized she'd lost a chance to connect with the woman. To nurture the fragile friendship that had gone off track when Delaney found out about YourMarket.

That didn't matter, either. In a couple of days, she'd never see Delaney Spencer again. "Whenever works for you," Maddie said through her suddenly thick throat. "Just let me know and I'll be here."

"How about later this morning?"

"Great. I'll see you then."

Maddie closed up the phone and headed upstairs to pack her clothes.

DELANEY ARRIVED a little after noon, with Paul, Jen and Jen's father, Al Horton, in tow. Fifteen minutes later, the desk was in place. The gleaming cherrywood looked even better in David's library than Maddie had imagined it would.

"It's beautiful," Jen said.

"Work of art, as usual. Delaney, you do damn good work," Al Horton said. Maddie hadn't met Jen's dad before, but she liked the gruff, friendly man.

"Thanks, Al," Delaney said easily. "I appreciate the delivery help."

"Least I could do, after you refinished those tables for me. Nell is thrilled with the way they turned out."

"Glad to hear it."

"Thanks, Dad." Jen looped her arm through her father's and steered him toward the front door. "Could you drop Paul off at Delaney's, so he can pick up his car?"

Al's bushy eyebrows rose. "Trying to get rid of me?"

"Not at all," Jen said. "You're more than welcome to stick around. Delaney and Maddie and I are going to talk about men and sex."

Al turned red. "Smart mouth," he muttered. He jerked his head at Paul. "Let's get out of here."

Maddie smiled as the two hurried out of the house. As the door slammed behind them, she stood at the desk, positioned just the way she'd imagined it. It fit the room perfectly. Just as David had known it would. Her smile disappeared.

"All right, Maddie. What's up?" Jen said from behind her.

"The Harp burned down last night." Maddie smoothed one hand over the desk. A faint scent of freshly cut wood clung to it. "That's what's up."

Jen sighed. "Besides that. Something happened with Quinn. Everyone was talking about it this morning at the Cherry Tree."

"No one gave you the details?" Maddie turned to face the two women. Delaney stood next to the big leather chair. Jen leaned against the wall. Both watched her carefully.

Delaney was the first to move. She slung an arm over Maddie's shoulder and steered her into the kitchen. "We want to hear your side of the story."

Maddie's eyes burned. "It's too humiliating to talk about."

"That's what girlfriends are for," Jen said, pushing her into one of the kitchen chairs. Delaney sat down, too, and Jen picked up the bottle of wine on the counter and pulled out the cork. "We need wine for this conversation."

She poured two glasses and passed one to Maddie. When she didn't ask Delaney if she wanted a glass, Maddie raised her eyebrows at the other woman. Delaney shook her head. "No, thanks."

"All right." Jen centered the wineglass in front of her. "Now we're ready to share your humiliation and plot revenge on the one who inflicted it."

It made Maddie cringe to think about telling them what had happened. But they might as well hear it from her.

"Quinn and I got into a fight." She slumped in the chair. "At the Harp, while it was burning."

"He was an idiot, wasn't he?" Jen said.

"He was upset."

Delaney cocked her head. "You're defending him?"

Maddie moved the wineglass on the wooden table. "No. What he did was... It was horrible," she finally said. "But I understood he was upset. It was just that it happened right after..."

She took a gulp of wine and pushed away from the table to stare, unseeing, out the window.

"You'd just made love," Delaney said quietly.

"How did you know?" Maddie asked.

"Many of the worst moments in a relationship come after sex," she said.

Maddie turned around, to find Delaney's expression closed. "You sound as if you speak from personal experience," she said lightly as she returned to the table.

Delaney got a glass of water. "I haven't spent my life in a convent. So what did he say?"

"Knowing Quinn, it was probably choice," Jen muttered wryly. She patted Maddie's hand. "He was scared."

"I was, too," Maddie admitted. She closed her eyes and fought to control the quaver in her voice. "This wasn't easy for me, either. My feelings for Quinn were all mixed up with how I feel about this house, the town, the pub. Business."

"Trust me, business had nothing to do with Quinn's reaction," Jen said. "He must have fallen hard for you."

"That's so comforting."

"I'm serious," Jen insisted. "I saw the way he looked at you. And he talked to you. Told you things."

"It was about sex and nothing more." Maddie took another sip of wine.

"You're the first woman he's dated since he moved back here," Delaney pointed out.

"And it took him less than two weeks to get me into bed. So not only am I a temporary resident, I'm easy, too." She took a gulp of wine. "Perfect, from his perspective."

"You're too hard on yourself," Jen said.

"She's not hard enough on Quinn," Delaney said.

"That, too."

"The next time I'm attracted to a man, I'm going to run the other way." Maddie stared at the dregs of wine left in her glass.

Jen nodded. "Always the smart thing to do."

"Just tell me one thing." Delaney leaned forward. "Was the sex at least fabulous?"

"Beyond fabulous," Maddie said with a sigh.

"That's too bad."

"No, it was too good." Maddie giggled and pushed her wineglass away. She'd wanted to be numb. To forget. But she'd had enough.

"Okay, now that we've decided Quinn is a bastard, let's move on to the revenge portion of the plan." Jen slapped her hands on the table.

"It sounds as if we're back in high school." Maddie glanced from her to Delaney. "Doesn't it?" She'd never talked about boys with her friends in high school. None of them ever had dates.

"Hey, you have to fight fire with fire," Jen said. "We've matured past revenge, but guys don't change. You have to hit them where it hurts. And we all know where that is, don't we?"

"It sure isn't their head," Delaney said, grinning.

Jen and Delaney were her friends. They'd come over to comfort her. To try to cheer her up. Why did everything have to fall apart now? Maddie wondered. Why did she have to leave Otter Tail just when she'd found them?

She swallowed the lump in her throat. "I almost feel sorry for him."

Fifteen minutes later, she finished telling them about the disastrous party and what had precipitated it.

"High school kids can be cruel," Jen said softly. "And we carry those scars for so long."

"What happened to you?" Maddie asked.

Jen shook her head. "Doesn't matter now. And I'm never going to see the guy again. Although, for the record, I was the mean one. What I did was horrible. And I've regretted it ever since."

"We've all done things we regret. I bet you have, too," Delaney said to Maddie.

"Of course I have. And publicly blurting out my teenage humiliation is right up there at the top of the list." She shook her head. "What's the matter with me? Why do I still care about what happened when I was sixteen?"

"We all have those moments, frozen in time, that we relive over and over," Delaney said.

"You want my opinion?" Jen asked gently. "Everyone will forget about what you said in a day or two. We hope you'll stay."

"Besides, we'll make Quinn suffer," Delaney assured her. "That's where the second part of the plan comes in. The revenge part."

"When a guy doesn't care, there's not much you can do for revenge," Maddie corrected her.

"He cares," Jen said. "Trust me. Otherwise he wouldn't have had that meltdown."

"So what are we going to do?" Delaney asked.

"I have an idea," Jen said, her eyes brightening.

"Yeah?" Delaney raised her brows. "Spill."

"Martha offered Quinn the Cherry Tree in the evenings. As a temporary Harp, so he still has money coming in." She glanced at Maddie. "I heard her say that he needs as much money as he can get to buy the land now."

"Martha? Martha offered to let him use her place? For free?" Delaney stared at Jen. "The same woman who won't give you a raise? The woman who rubs her pennies together until they scream for mercy? Did aliens abduct her and put a pod person in her place?"

"I couldn't believe it, either. But I heard her talking to him." She smiled. "So here's what we do."

## CHAPTER NINETEEN

IT TOOK TWO DAYS to transform the Cherry Tree Diner into the Harp South, as everyone was calling it. It seemed as if the whole town had pitched in to help—everyone but Maddie. Maddie, Jen and Delaney had decided she needed to stay away from Quinn until the temporary Harp opened.

She'd kept busy talking to the insurance company and examining the burned out pub with the adjusters. She hoped it wouldn't take too long for them to send a check.

But whenever she managed to put the pub and her finances out of her head, Quinn was waiting in the wings. A fresh wave of pain swept over her every time she thought of him.

In her sane moments, Maddie wondered what the heck she was doing. Why had she let Jen and Delaney talk her into their scheme?

It was clear Quinn was no longer interested. The hours that passed without a phone call just underlined his words. He was a player—excited by the chase, bored when he caught his prey. Maddie should salvage her pride and forget about him.

She didn't want to forget about him. She couldn't quite extinguish that last tiny flicker of hope.

And Jen's plan would be satisfying. Show the player what he'd lost. Torment him with the vision of what had once been his.

Maddie paused at the door of the diner, smoothing down her skirt. She could do this. She'd smile until her face ached, flirt with every guy, and ignore Quinn.

Juvenile? Yes. High school? Absolutely.

But she was a desperate woman. She hadn't been able to come up with anything better. So she'd give it a try.

She opened the door of the Cherry Tree and took a deep breath.

Some tables had been stacked and pushed into a corner, leaving an open space in the middle of the restaurant, which was crowded with customers. The booths against the walls were all occupied. Bins of ice filled with bottles of beer stood on the floor behind the counter, and Quinn was ringing up sales as fast as he could. A line of people waited patiently to buy a drink. Jen had offered to cook until nine o'clock, and Maddie could see her moving around in the kitchen.

It looked as if everyone in Otter Tail was there. All to support Quinn.

Ignoring the lump in her throat, Maddie grabbed an apron from behind the counter. Quinn stopped her before she could get to work.

"What are you doing here?"

She shook off his hand. "I work here. Or did you fire me?"

He let her go and studied her, his eyes narrowed. "I didn't think you'd show up."

She wouldn't have, if Jen and Delaney hadn't pushed

her. "I've never quit a job without giving notice, and I'm not going to start just because my…supervisor is a jerk." She gave him a cool smile. "Besides, I need the money."

QUINN WAITED for her to say more. What was Maddie up to? Why would she want to work, after what he'd said to her?

He had all night to figure it out.

"Fine. You should make good tips tonight."

Out of the corner of his eye, he saw Sam Talbott signaling for a beer. Quinn reached down and pulled a dripping longneck out of the bin. "We're only serving wine and beer," he said, wiping the bottle off, opening it and handing it to Sam. "That container's domestic, the other imported. You can get the beer yourself. I'll pour the wine. There's more beer in the refrigerator out back, and there are trash cans around the room for the bottles. Let me know when they need to be emptied."

"Right." She tied the apron around her waist, then got to work. He stared after her until Paul waved his hand in front of Quinn's face.

"Don't suppose you have any cans of Guinness?"

"Nope." Quinn rattled off the brands he had.

"Give me a Leinie, then." Paul leaned on the counter. "I'm surprised to see Maddie here."

Quinn twisted the cap of the Leinenkugel's off with a little more force than necessary. "She works here."

"I heard what you said to her the other night. Not one of your best moves, Murphy."

"I was pissed off."

"Sounded like it. Have you fixed it yet?"

"Fixed what?" Quinn gave his friend a hard stare.

Paul took a long swig of his beer. "You're pathetic," he finally said. "Have you even talked to her?"

Scowling, Quinn poured a glass of wine for Laura Taylor. "I've been busy."

"Looks like she's been busy, too."

"What?" He set the bottle down with a thud and searched for her. She was talking to Augie. Smiling. She patted him on the shoulder and walked away.

Quinn caught a flash of leg and looked more closely. She was wearing that damn skirt.

*"Next time, I won't wear any underwear."* He stared at her rear end.

"She does have a nice ass," Paul said.

Quinn swung around on him. "Stay away from Maddie's ass."

"Hey, you can't look after your toys, they get taken away." Paul sauntered off, drinking his beer.

*Smart-ass.* But Maddie sure as hell was acting as if she had forgotten all about him.

She sidled between two men and bent to get two Leinies out of the bin. When she stood, her gaze met Quinn's.

"What?" She bent to pull out two more beers.

"You know damn well *what.*" He jerked his chin at her skirt. "That."

"What about it?"

"Why are you wearing it?"

She raised her eyebrows. "Because it's comfortable. And I get more tips."

"Damn it, Maddie, that's not why you wore it."

"Really? You can read my mind now?"

He clenched his jaw. "Don't wear it to work again."

"You didn't have a problem with it the other night."

"I've changed my mind."

"Too bad. I've decided I like wearing skirts." She gave him a saucy smile. "They're nice and breezy."

She grabbed the four beers.

*Breezy.* He watched the swing of her hips as she walked away, and shifted uncomfortably. He didn't need this tonight.

A few minutes later, Delaney leaned on the counter. "Have any soda back there, Quinn?"

"Yeah." He tore his gaze away from Maddie. "What do you want?"

"Anything without caffeine," Delaney said. "Any more, and I won't be responsible for my actions."

He slid a can of 7up across to her. "How's that?"

"Good." She popped the top and took a drink as she studied him. "You look all pissed off about something. I thought you'd be happy with everyone turning out for you."

Quinn saw how her eyes were twinkling, and muttered, "Go to hell, Delaney."

Laughing, she took another drink of her soda and left him.

Maddie was talking to Jen now. When Delaney joined them, all three women glanced at him. He heard Jen laugh.

He turned away, fuming. And aroused. Every time he looked at Maddie in that skirt, he got harder.

By the time the Harp South clientele began to thin out, he was aching for Maddie. She had ignored him, except when she had to ask for a glass of wine.

Someone at the back of the room signaled for a drink. As Maddie made her way toward the guy, the stereo system blared a country song about a cowboy who wanted to pick ticks off his girlfriend. Quinn wanted to throw something at the damn boom box. The last thing he needed to hear tonight was a song about some guy kissing his girlfriend in the moonlight.

Paul was the one who'd been signaling for a beer. Instead of returning for his drink, Maddie stood and chatted with him.

Quinn closed his fingers into a fist as Paul smiled at her. When Maddie smiled back, he turned away.

A few minutes later, she grabbed another beer out of the bin. Quinn couldn't stop himself from saying, "Having a good time with the customers?"

She wiped the bottle with the cloth hanging from the counter. "Isn't that what I'm supposed to do? Talk to people? Be friendly? No one likes a grumpy waitress." She grinned. "Just like no one likes a grumpy bartender."

When there were only a few customers left, Maddie started cleaning up. The citrus smell of her hair taunted him every time she got close. He remembered that smell from when he'd held her. From when they'd made love.

Finally, when only Paul was left in the diner, she hung up her apron. "You had a good night," she said as she grabbed her purse and slung it over her shoulder. "Congratulations."

"You sticking around?" he heard himself ask.

She looked at him. "Why would I do that, Quinn?"

"To help me celebrate, maybe?"

For a moment, he thought he saw a light in her eyes. Then, when he didn't say anything more, the spark died. "I'm guessing you'll manage to celebrate just fine on your own."

As she disappeared through the door, he wanted to run out and call her back. He missed talking to her after the pub closed, missed watching her eyes when she laughed about something that had happened that night.

He missed looking at her legs in that skirt.

He couldn't pretend he was calling her back about work—she'd done everything she was supposed to do and more. She'd carried empty bottles out to the recycling, helped set up the tables so the restaurant could open the next morning, and helped clean the kitchen. There was nothing left to do.

He wouldn't ask her to stay just because he liked having her around. Hell, if he did, she'd probably punch him.

But she'd worn the skirt. Had it been a signal of some sort? Was she trying to tell him something?

"For someone who just sold a butt load of beer and wine, you don't look very happy."

"Paul." Quinn narrowed his eyes as his friend slid onto a stool at the counter. "What are you still doing here?"

"I thought you could use some help, closing up the restaurant."

"Thanks," Quinn said, trying to smile. "But I think it's covered."

Paul reached over the counter and grabbed a beer. "So you didn't ask Maddie to stick around."

"No reason to. The work is done."

Paul raised his eyebrows. "Oh, I could think of some reasons besides work."

"Name one."

"You have some groveling to do. You might as well get it over with."

"Why would I grovel to Maddie?"

"Because you treated her badly and you have something going with her, maybe?"

"That's over."

"Really? You sure about that?"

She *had* worn the skirt to work. "Did she say something to you? About me?"

"This isn't high school, buddy. If you want to know what Maddie said to me, ask her yourself."

"Why do you think it's not over?" Quinn pressed.

"Maybe because, for some unknown reason, she seems to like your company. Me, I can't see it, but who can tell with women?"

Quinn slumped against the wall. "Not anymore, she doesn't."

"That's what happens when you tell a woman to get lost, in front of an audience." Paul drank his beer before adding quietly, "She scared you, didn't she?"

"You know my deal. I don't do relationships."

"Oh, that makes perfect sense. A woman falls into your life—a gorgeous, funny, smart woman—who seems to be crazy about you. You can't keep your hands off her. Yeah, I'd tell her to get lost, too."

His skull was beginning to pound. "Leave it alone, Paul."

"The hell. Someone needs to pull your head out of

your ass, and I'm electing myself. It's time to move on, Quinn. Time to rejoin the world. And that includes having a normal, healthy relationship."

"I'm not interested." Quinn dumped the ice from one of the buckets into the sink. He'd just screw it up, anyway. Or hurt Maddie even more, which he wouldn't be able to bear. "That's why I got rid of Maddie."

"You are friggin' out of your mind, pal. Get your act together. Tell her you temporarily lost it. Get her back."

"I don't want Maddie."

"You sure?"

"Positive."

"Great. Then you won't mind if I ask her out." Paul popped off the stool. "I've had my eye on her since the first time I saw her."

Quinn froze. "You go near her and I'll take your head off," he snarled at his friend.

"You can't have it both ways." Paul opened the door. "Make up your mind, Quinn."

The bell on the door tinkled as it closed behind him.

# CHAPTER TWENTY

MADDIE SAT ON THE screened porch and nibbled at a sandwich. She'd hoped the scenery would distract her, but even the bright moon rising over the lake couldn't take her mind off the evening. She shouldn't have gone into work. She'd ended up tormenting herself far more than she'd upset Quinn.

A car turned into her driveway, and she tensed. There hadn't been a repeat of the spray-painted vulgarity on the front porch, or the broken light, but no one came for a visit at this time of night.

A car door slammed, and she relaxed a little. Whoever was here wasn't trying to be quiet. Setting her plate on the table, she got up and walked to the entryway.

Quinn stood on her porch.

She opened the door. "What are you doing here?"

"You fixed the broken light and planted flowers in front of the house."

"It's almost one in the morning. Not exactly the time for a garden tour."

"I came to thank you for working tonight." He stared at her chest.

"Eyes up here," she said.

He lifted his head, his cheeks red. "Department of Redundancy Department." He nodded at her shirt. "I like clever. I was appreciating the T-shirt."

"I'll bet you were." As she waited, he seemed unsure of himself. Awkward. Maybe he wanted to apologize and couldn't find the words. "You didn't have to come all the way out here to thank me for working. I keep my commitments."

His jaw tightened. "Go ahead and say it, Maddie. Tell me I don't."

She opened her eyes wide. "What are you talking about? You never made any commitments to me. Other than to pay me for working at the Harp. Which you've done." She smiled brightly. "So we're good, aren't we?"

"Can I come in?" he asked.

She studied him for a moment, but couldn't read him. "Fine." She stepped aside, her heart racing. "Come into the library."

It was hard to have him in her house. But they'd never kissed in the library. Never touched each other. At least here she wouldn't have to battle memories of what they'd done.

He headed for the desk by the window. "That's new. Did Delaney make it?" He ran his hand over the wood.

A memory of the way he'd touched Maddie flashed through her mind, but she shoved it away. "Yes. David ordered it before…" She swallowed. "Before he died."

"It's beautiful."

"Yes, it is."

"What made him order a desk when he was so sick with cancer?"

"He didn't tell me," she said. Yet again she regretted that David hadn't told her about his leukemia. He'd known she was consumed with the mess she'd made of her life, and she knew him well enough to know he'd wanted to spare her. But hell would freeze over before she shared with Quinn any more intimate details of her life. "What did you want to talk to me about?"

He turned and leaned against the desk. "Some of those plants in front of the house are perennials. Does that mean you're sticking around Otter Tail for a while?"

"What difference does it make?"

He stared at her for a long time. "I need to know if I should hire someone for the Harp," he finally said.

"I'll give you notice if I'm going to quit."

"You don't have to quit." It sounded almost like a plea. "It won't bother me to have you working there."

"You've already made that clear," she said coolly. "I got it the first time."

"Damn it, Maddie, I didn't mean it like that." He scowled. "I know you need the money. You make good tips at the Harp."

"You're offering me a pity job? Kind of like your pity screw down on the beach?"

"It wasn't like that." He stepped closer. She thought he was going to grab her, and she was disappointed when he clenched his hands at his sides. "For God's sake, Maddie. We could have fun if you stayed." He glanced at the pajama pants hiding her legs. "I spent the whole damn evening trying to figure out if you were naked beneath that skirt."

"What are you saying, Quinn?" A fist curled around

her heart and squeezed so tightly that she thought she'd crumple from the pain. She'd assumed he'd come over to apologize. Instead, he'd come over looking for sex.

"I figured you wore that skirt for a reason. To send a signal."

"What signal would that be?" It took every ounce of her strength to lean casually against the wall, as if she was merely curious. As if she wasn't dying inside.

He shoved his hands through his hair. "That we were, you know, okay. That you wanted the same thing I did."

"And that would be...?"

"Come on, Maddie. Do I have to spell it out?"

"I think you do." She wrapped her arms around herself. "To have a good time until you leave."

"No-strings sex," she said, her voice flat.

"You had a good time, too," he replied defensively.

Did he know, at some level, that she wanted to slug him?

*A good time.* Her chest hurt so much, she was surprised she could breathe. "Who are you, Quinn?"

"What kind of question is that?"

"I thought I knew you. You lied about David. What else did you lie about?"

"What do you mean, I lied about David?" He was genuinely bewildered.

"You told me he was your best friend." She stepped away from the support of the wall. She had to put more space between herself and Quinn. "David wouldn't have been friends with someone like you. Someone who just wants to use people."

He flinched. "What the hell do you know about David

and what he did or wanted? You never came to see him, not even when he was sick. Or for his funeral." Quinn stalked over to her, but she held her ground. "He talked about you all the time. You were the most important person in the world to him. And you couldn't be bothered to visit him before he died. Or show up to bury him."

She pressed her hand to her chest, but he didn't notice.

"Do you think David would have wanted you to sell the Harp to YourMarket? To rip out Otter Tail's heart like that? He would have told you to let the past go. To forget about revenge. To move beyond what happened here when you were a kid. So don't tell me what David would have wanted. You don't have a clue."

"You think that's why I considered YourMarket? Did you listen to *anything* I told you? I need money. Lots of it. Revenge has nothing to do with it."

She shoved him, catching him by surprise, and he stumbled backward. "And 'let the past go'? Like you have?" She shoved him again. "You're wallowing in the past. Keeping it as close as a lover. No wonder you can't get involved. Paul wants you to run for mayor, and you'd be perfect for the job. But you'll never do it. Not in a million years. Because you're a coward who's afraid of getting hurt again."

She kicked the floor lamp next to the couch, then hid a grimace of pain. "You go ahead and have a pity party. Go ahead and hide in your pub. If you want to live your life alone, I'm not going to try and change your mind. But don't tell me about what David would want. Because he sure as hell wouldn't know who you are."

"You have no idea what you're talking about."

"Is that right?" She drew herself taller and stared Quinn down. "Convince me I'm wrong."

His expression was tight. But he didn't say anything, and suddenly her eyes prickled and her head ached as much as her heart.

"I thought what you did the other night when the pub was burning was bad. This is ten times worse—coming over here to ask for sex when I thought you were going to apologize to me. Get out."

He rubbed the back of his neck. "It's not like that, Maddie, and you know it."

"Do I? I thought I knew a lot of things. Turns out I was wrong." She'd lost all desire to fight with him. She strode to the front door and opened it. "I changed my mind. I'm giving you notice. I can't be around you. I'll work for another week, to give you a chance to find someone else, but that's it."

"Don't quit."

"Why not? So you can spend your evenings looking at my ass and wondering if I'm wearing panties?"

"Maddie, you're deliberately misunderstanding me."

"No, I think I understand you perfectly." She opened the door wider. "Good night, Quinn."

He stood there for a long moment, frustration and hunger written on his face. Then he stormed out the door. "Don't wear that skirt again."

"I'll wear anything I damn well please."

THE TOWN WAS DESERTED as Quinn drove back. He pulled over to the side of the road and stopped in front of the Harp. *I thought I knew you, but I don't know you at all.* What was she talking about? They knew each other as well as two people could.

He stared at the ruins of his pub. He needed to get a grip, to figure out how to put the pieces of his life back together, but all he could think about was Maddie. *You're a coward who's afraid of getting hurt again.*

Only a fool made the same mistakes more than once. He knew better than to let down his guard. He knew where it could lead.

When dawn was a hint of light on the horizon, he reached into the glove box and pulled out a flashlight. Then he walked across the street to the Harp.

It smelled of wet, burned wood and acrid smoke. The shattered front window opened into inky darkness. It was probably unsafe as hell in there.

Quinn stepped through the window and switched on his flashlight. Skeletons of chairs lay on their sides, shoved into piles with the tables from the force of the fire hoses. The granite bar he'd found in an old pub in Milwaukee was cracked and blackened. Some of the shelves of liquor bottles had fallen, littering the area behind the bar with broken glass. The cupboards above the mirror were either hanging crookedly or had fallen altogether. The top two shelves were intact, however. The glass in some of the doors was missing, but bottles fogged from the heat were still lined up there, the last ghostly reminders of normalcy.

He made his way through the debris to the kitchen. The damage wasn't as severe here; stainless steel didn't burn as easily as wood. His light picked out the grill, the freezer, the refrigerator. All looked relatively untouched. Maybe they could be salvaged if—

Nope, the Harp was gone. All that was left to do was to sweep up the remains and carry them away.

As he aimed the flashlight behind the bar, he saw his old bottle of Jameson in the middle cupboard. Untouched. Glass crunched beneath his shoes as he walked behind the ruined bar, reached up and took it down.

The bottle felt gritty, but it was still half-full. He remembered the bite of the whiskey in his mouth, remembered how it had washed his memories into oblivion.

*You're wallowing in the past.*

He tightened his grip around the neck of the bottle, then made his way outside.

## CHAPTER TWENTY-ONE

A CAR DOOR SLAMMED in his driveway, and Quinn stirred.

As he lifted his head from the kitchen table, the first thing he saw was the bottle of Jameson he'd set there the night before. Still half-full.

He'd done it. On one of the worst nights of his life, he hadn't taken a drink.

It had been a struggle, but the whiskey was still here. And so was he.

Someone pounded on his door. Quinn took a deep breath, his heart suddenly racing. "What?"

"Open the door, Murphy."

"Get lost, Paul." Quinn slumped into his seat again. Had he really thought it would be Maddie?

"Not going to happen. I need to tell you something." The door thumped in its frame, and Quinn realized Paul had settled against it.

Quinn shoved his chair backward. He flung the door open and Paul fell in. "You're a pain in the ass, Black."

"So you've said." Paul looked around the room and stilled when he spotted the Jameson. "Aw, damn it, Quinn."

"It's not what it looks like," he said.

"No? You were sleeping with the bottle, for God's sake. The imprint of the kitchen table is still on your face."

"I didn't take a drink."

Paul shrugged. "Not my business if you want to kill yourself. Some people might be upset, though."

"No, she wouldn't." Quinn threw himself back into his chair.

Paul pulled up another and sat down, while Quinn scrubbed his face with his hands. It felt as if all the dust and smoke from the Harp had settled in his eyes. He closed them tight. "I screwed up," he finally said. He'd stared at the bottle for hours until he'd understood.

"Hey, you're making progress. That's more than you knew last night." There was no blame or censure in Paul's voice.

"Yeah. I'm real smart. Quick, too."

"So you're a slow learner. Maddie might decide you're trainable."

Quinn stared out the window, to see the sun was high in the sky. It had to be past noon, and he wondered what she was doing. "I was a jerk again last night," he said quietly. "I hurt her."

"At the Harp?" Paul asked. "I doubt she noticed you watching her rear end."

"She noticed. But that's not what I'm talking about."

"What, then?"

Quinn told his friend what he'd done.

"I have to hand it to you, Quinn," Paul said when he'd finished. "When you screw up, it's not a half-assed effort. So what are you going to do about it?"

"Apologize." Knowing Maddie, she'd probably slam the door in his face.

"And then…?"

"Then what?"

"What are you going to do after you apologize?" Paul said patiently. "For God's sake, Quinn. You don't think you're going to waltz in, tell Maddie you're sorry, and it'll be all hearts and flowers again, do you?"

Yeah, he had. "Um, tell her I'm a jerk?"

"Trust me, she already knows. Are you going to make some kind of commitment to her? Is that what she wants? Is it what you want?"

"How the hell should I know?" he answered. "It took me all night to figure this much out." It felt as if every one of his nerves was exposed. "What did you come over here for, anyway? You said you had to tell me something."

Paul studied him for a moment, then nodded. Clearly, he realized that they were done with all the touchy-feely crap. "Cal Hodges has been trying to call you. He got worried when you didn't answer your phone."

Quinn pulled his phone out of his pocket. "Not charged."

"Yeah, I figured. I volunteered to come out and make sure you were okay."

"Why wouldn't I be okay?"

"God knows. Your life is perfect right now. You own a thriving business and you're in a relationship with a great woman. Come on, Quinn." Paul nodded at the bottle of Jameson. "Everyone knows you used to be a drinker. No one would be shocked if you'd started again."

*I can't bear to be around you.*

Quinn touched the bottle, then stood up. "Why was Cal trying to get hold of me?"

"They know who burned down your pub." Quinn spun around to face Paul. "And they're pretty sure they know where to find him."

"Tell me."

"Someone reported a prowler near J. D. Stroger's house, and they found a gas can in J.D.'s garbage."

"J.D.? Really? He's an obnoxious drunk, but I didn't figure him for burning the Harp down."

"It wasn't him. It was Andre." Paul shook his head. "You have to give the little bastard credit. He knew J.D. had trouble the last couple times he was in the Harp. That's why Andre threw the can in his garbage. But the dumbass didn't wipe the can down. His fingerprints were all over it."

"They haven't arrested him?"

"His wife kicked him out after you fired him, and someone said he was staying with a cousin in Sturgeon Falls. Cal sent Jed Miller to check it out."

The Harp was gone because of an angry, vindictive employee. "Thanks for letting me know." Quinn opened the refrigerator and stared inside to signal that it was time for Paul to leave.

His friend didn't take the hint. "Have you contacted your insurance agent yet?"

"Yeah, I called her the next day." Quinn slammed the refrigerator door. "She said I'd be getting a check soon for the equipment and furnishings. Maddie will get a sum for the building, since she's the owner." He'd give his check to Maddie in an instant as a down payment for the land, but he suspected that option was gone.

"There's talk in town about holding a recall election to get rid of Gordon. People are pissed off about Your-Market, and they know he wants them to set up shop in town. You should run for mayor."

"I can't be mayor," Quinn said automatically.

"Why not?"

"I wouldn't know what to do."

Paul shrugged. "It's not that tough. You can learn on the job. The only requirement is caring about this town. About the people. And you do. You're a leader. People listen to you."

He was a leader? "That's not my thing."

"What *is* your thing? Sitting alone in your house, drinking?"

"I don't drink anymore." The Jameson would always call to him, but he was done answering. "I'm sure you can come up with a better choice. Why don't you run? You're involved in everything in Otter Tail."

"Can't do that," Paul said. "My job is to fight the man. If I'm the mayor, I *am* the man."

"You're a barrel of laughs."

"Think about it." Paul opened the door. "I'll see you tonight at the Harp South, right?"

"I'll be there." Where else would he be?

The sound of Paul's car faded away into silence. Quinn's neck was stiff and it felt as if the Russian army had marched through his mouth in their socks. He was getting too old to fall asleep at the kitchen table.

After showering and shaving, he felt only marginally

better. Maddie's face haunted him. He couldn't forget her shattered expression when she'd realized he'd just been looking for sex.

He had to make things right with her. He needed to apologize.

He needed to know if she truly believed in second chances.

THE SUN BURNED her shoulders and waves of heat reflected off the asphalt as Maddie struggled up the hill on County U. Even the pine-scented air tasted flat, like a glass of water left sitting on the counter too long.

Stupid to go for a run. She had too many other things to do. But she was addicted, and her addiction had to be fed.

Better to satisfy her craving for running than her old dependence on food.

She shouldn't have picked this hill, though. It was where Quinn had found her that day. Bet her she couldn't beat him. Suckered her into working at the Harp.

What was wrong with her? Why had she come this way?

She was a glutton for punishment.

Stupid, on top of that, to save the hill for the end of her run, when her muscles were already burning. But then, she had done a lot of things backward since she'd come to Otter Tail. Like fall in love with a man, then find out who he really was.

She heard the low rumble of an engine behind her and moved to the shoulder of the road. She stepped on a stone and felt a sharp pang as her ankle twisted, but she didn't slow down.

She didn't want company right now. She didn't want to have to smile and be sociable.

Instead of accelerating to pass her, though, the car slowed. She glanced over her shoulder and her heart stuttered at the sight of Quinn's truck.

He pulled up beside her and leaned out the window. "You're still running without water." He held a bottle out the window. It was misty with condensation, and she realized how thirsty she was. She'd been trying to outrun her pain and had headed out without thinking.

"Take it, Maddie," he said when he saw her hesitate. "I didn't poison it."

She bit back the sharp retort she wanted to make, and took the bottle. "Thank you." She unscrewed the cap and drank deeply.

"You need a keeper," Quinn said when she'd finished.

She was sure he wasn't volunteering for the job. "I'll put up a notice on Craigslist," she said, pleased at how cool her voice sounded.

"Smart-ass." Quinn jumped out of his truck and she backed into the shade of the trees lining the road. No sense in broiling in the sun.

"How did you know where I was?"

"I went to your house. When you weren't there, I went into the Cherry Tree and asked if anyone had seen you. Jen saw you go by in your running shorts." He looked down at the hill she'd just climbed. "I followed your regular route."

Maddie shrugged, as if she had forgotten all about

their last encounter here. "It's the best place around for a challenging run."

He stood in front of her, blocking her way. If she wanted to leave, she'd have to push him aside. Since she didn't want to touch him, she'd have to talk to him. "What do you want, Quinn?"

"A couple of things. First, I don't care what Paul says, I didn't drink the Jameson."

"What are you talking about? I haven't seen Paul since last night at the Harp South."

He sighed. "I should have kept my mouth shut. But Paul is such a do-gooder, I figured he'd tell you."

"What about the Jameson?"

"It's not important."

"Since you brought it up, I think it is."

He rubbed a hand over his face. "I took my bottle of Jameson home with me."

She instinctively reached out to him, then dropped her hand when she realized what she'd done. "Why?"

"It's the bottle I was working on when I quit drinking. I kept it at the Harp. On the top shelf. To remind me. I figured if I could get through last night without taking a drink, I could handle anything."

"And did you?"

"Yeah." He held her gaze, and she couldn't look away. "But I was tempted. Sometimes oblivion is attractive."

"I know all about needing to forget."

"When have you ever needed oblivion?"

She wiped the sweat from the side of her face with one arm and looked at him wearily. "I was a fat girl, Quinn. I ate because it made me feel good, when nothing else in my life did. My mother didn't really want a kid. I couldn't control that. She made me come up here in the summer, and I couldn't control that, either. But I could control what I ate."

Birds chattered in the trees behind them and a cow lowed in the distance. "Thank you for telling me that," he said quietly.

She lifted one shoulder. "You're not the only one who has baggage."

She tried to push past him, but he stepped in front of her. "Don't go."

"Why not? Did you come to tell me you didn't take a drink last night, even though you were tempted? Good for you. That's great. But you need to get your attaboys from your mentor at AA. Not me."

"God, you're tough." He shoved his hair off his forehead. "That's not why I was looking for you. I'm not even sure why I told you about the Jamesons, except that I figured Paul said something."

Maybe because he wanted to share more of himself with her? Forget it. Quinn had been very clear about where he stood on intimacy. "You said there were a couple of things." She stretched one leg, then the other. To show she was ready to start running again. That she knew this was just a minor break in her routine.

Quinn's eyes darkened as he watched her, then he lifted his gaze. "I came to apologize for last night. I hurt you. Again. That's the last thing I want to do."

"Really? Seemed like that was exactly what you were trying to do. Especially the night the Harp burned down."

"I was scared, Maddie," he said in a low voice. "Of what I felt for you. About you. What I wanted."

Her heart began to pound. "Really? And what was that? Besides more sex."

"You're not going to let me forget that, are you?"

The memory was too fresh to ignore. "It does seem to be the theme running through our relationship. Oh, sorry, you don't do those, do you? I guess I should have said our booty call."

"Can you stop with the smart mouth? I'm trying to make things right here," he said quietly. "I'm trying to say I'm sorry."

Her smart mouth was the only way she could protect herself. "Is that it?"

"No." He reached out a hand as if to touch her, then let it drop. "I want a second chance with you, Maddie. I want to figure out how to make this work."

"What is *this?*"

"You're going to make me say it, aren't you?" When she didn't answer, he shoved his hand through his hair again. "The thing is, I think I could fall in love with you. I think we could have a relationship. Or more."

He *thought* he could fall in love with her? What had the past few weeks been about, if not falling in love with each other?

"You make it sound as if it's a distasteful chore." She focused on a bird's nest in a tree. An empty one. It looked tattered and sad, as if it had been abandoned long ago. "The thing is, Quinn, I *am* in love with you. And I'm not willing to settle for maybes. Maybe you could love me? *Maybe* we could have a future together? I can't give you my heart and hope you don't reject me again." She took a deep breath. "I'm going back to Chicago. I have to get my life there straightened out. My friend Hollis needs her money, and I got the check from the insurance company today. That will pay what I owe her. But I still have to settle with the contractors."

"You love me, but you won't let me make this right? You won't let me fix what I did?" There was an edge of desperation in Quinn's voice.

"I don't have a choice." Every fiber of her wanted to stay. Wanted to throw herself at Quinn. But she was worth more than that. "I can't force you to care about me. I've tried to do that too many times in my life, and I'm not doing it again."

"So you're running."

"What can I say? It's what I do best."

"Then all that talk about everyone deserving a second chance was just crap. Something you said to make me feel better, but didn't really mean."

She'd meant it. She just didn't know if she could do it. "You hurt me, Quinn. Badly. I know when to stop throwing myself at a guy and move on."

"What if I ask you not to go?"

She waited for a long time, but he didn't say anything else. "You'll have to do better than that."

"I want you, Maddie."

She pushed past him, her heart crumbling in her chest. "I want you, too, Quinn. But you know what? That's not enough. I want a lot of things that aren't good for me. And right now, you're just another thing I have to avoid."

## CHAPTER TWENTY-TWO

"SELL IT TO QUINN for $100,000," Maddie said to Laura.

There was silence from the other end of the phone. "Are you sure?" the Realtor finally asked. "You could get at least $150,000 for the land."

"No, I want Quinn to have it."

Laura cleared her throat. "I thought you needed more money."

"I do." Maddie looked down at the check on her kitchen counter. "I got the cash from the insurance company for the building, and that will help. I'll get the rest when…" Her throat closed and she struggled to compose herself. "When you sell the house," she said. "Put it up for sale."

"The house? Aren't you going to live there?" Laura asked.

"My plans changed. I'm heading back to Chicago."

"Really? What about Quinn?"

Maddie blinked rapidly as she stared out the window. That's what happened when you lived in a small town. There were no secrets. "I'm not staying in Otter Tail."

"Oh. Well, then, I'll need to come out and take a look at the house."

"I'll drop the key off on my way out of town."

"That soon?"

"Yes." Better to make a clean break to minimize the pain. "I'll see you this afternoon." Maddie flipped her phone closed.

She traced her finger over the writing on the check from Eversure Insurance Company and told herself she was stupid to feel so bereft. She should be happy. Her most immediate problem was solved—Hollis would be able to repay her IRA. There would even be a little left over for the most delinquent of Maddie's contractor bills.

When the house sold, she could pay off the rest of her debts.

But all she felt was sorrow.

She folded the check carefully, put it into her wallet and set her purse next to the front door. Alongside the rest of her belongings, waiting to be loaded into her SUV.

She wasn't running away. She had business back in Chicago. Things she needed to do. She wanted to see Hollis—her friendship with Delaney and Jen had reminded her how much she missed her old friend.

Maddie walked through the house again to make sure she wasn't leaving anything behind. She finished in the library, and her eyes went to David's desk. Maybe, once she found a place in Chicago, she'd drive back here and pick it up.

David had meant it for her, after all. He'd wanted her to have it.

He'd meant for her to live with it in this house.

The desk belonged here, even if she didn't. Every choice came with a sacrifice.

She sat in the chair she'd pulled up to it and stared out the window. At the view she wouldn't see while she was working. She wouldn't watch the seasons change.

The surface of the desk was like glass beneath her fingers. She pictured David, writing down what she'd said about desks. Talking to Delaney about making it.

She pulled out the first drawer, and it slid open quietly and effortlessly. The scent of freshly cut wood drifted up to her. One by one, she opened all the drawers, imagining what she would have put into each of them. Imagining David doing the same as he designed it.

A piece of brown leather sat in the bottom drawer, and she reached down for it. Delaney must have accidentally left something in the desk.

As Maddie pulled it out, she stilled. This hadn't been left by mistake.

She set the leather carefully on top of the desk and unrolled it. It was a small tool belt holding a hammer, four screwdrivers, a pair of pliers and a ruler. The tool belt David had given her the first summer she'd spent in Otter Tail.

The hammer stuck in its loop when she tried to pull it out. Just like it always had. The head was rough from pounding countless nails into countless pieces of wood. At the beginning, most of them had gone in crooked, but David had shown her how to pull the nail out and start over. By the last summer she'd been in Otter Tail, she'd been able to drive a nail straight and true.

The smaller of the Phillips head screwdrivers wasn't ever going to work right. She'd worn away the ridges, trying to use it on the wrong-sized screws. The larger of the flat-head screwdrivers had a chunk missing from the handle. One of her earliest attempts to use the hammer had gone awry.

Every year, she'd asked David if she could bring them home with her when she left for the summer. David had always told her that they belonged in Otter Tail, so they'd be waiting for her when she returned.

Maddie leaned back in her chair and looked at the remnants of her childhood as she wiped away tears. David had given her the tools, but they represented so much more that he'd given her. Love. Possibilities. A sense of belonging.

She replaced them in the tool belt and folded it carefully. The desk needed to stay, but the tool belt was going with her.

It took less than fifteen minutes to load her car, check the house one more time and lock it up. She stared at the key, hanging on the tarnished red cherry key chain that said Door County. David had used that key chain for as long as she could remember.

She slid the key off and put the keychain into her pocket. She would take that back with her, too.

The house fairly glowed in the sunlight, and she memorized every detail as she stood in the front yard. The bleeding hearts and peonies she'd planted were bright splashes of color against the yellow house.

They added to the curb appeal. Maybe the place would sell faster.

By the time she got to Laura's, she'd managed to swallow her tears. She handed the real estate agent the key, gave her a hug and got back in her car as fast as she could. Maddie focused on the road as she headed south on County S. She didn't want a last look at Otter Tail. She was carrying enough memories with her.

*Give me a second chance.*

That one would be the hardest to forget.

As she passed the last house and flashed past fields of soybeans, she glanced at the passenger seat, where she'd put the tool belt. David's voice whispered through her head. "With the right tools, you can fix anything."

She stared at the road through suddenly blurry eyes. Did she have the tools to fix what had gone wrong in her life?

She didn't want to leave. She wanted to stay in Otter Tail. She wanted to make a life with Quinn.

So why was she leaving?

Because she was scared. As scared as he was.

Just as afraid to take a chance.

She eased her foot off the accelerator. She was protecting herself as much as Quinn had been.

She didn't want to live in Chicago. She wanted to live in Otter Tail. With him.

Gravel crunched beneath her tires as she pulled onto the shoulder of the road and stopped. She stared at the endless field of soybeans. Was she really thinking about going back? About opening herself to rejection, taking the chance of being hurt again?

Could she do it?

That's what David would have told her to do.

She took a deep breath and turned the car around.

Her hands shook as she accelerated.

She was going to fight for the life she wanted.

She was driving way too fast when a black truck flew past her. She glanced in the rearview mirror, then slammed on her brakes.

It was Quinn.

He slowed down. Turned around. Pulled up behind her SUV.

As she got out, her legs trembled. So did her hands. She hid them behind her back.

Quinn leaped out of the truck and slammed the door. "Where are you going?" he asked.

"I was headed to Chicago."

"You're driving the wrong way. Did you forget something?"

"Yes, I did. I was going back for it." She shoved her hands into the back pockets of her jeans.

"What did you forget, Maddie?" He moved in close.

She took a deep breath and jumped off the cliff. "I forgot you. I thought I was being strong by walking away, but I don't want to leave you, Quinn. I want that second chance you asked for."

"Are you sure?"

"Yes. I love you. I'll give you all the time you need to figure this out."

"You think I can change?"

"If you want something enough, you can do anything."

He reached for her hands and intertwined their fingers. "Ask me what I was doing out here, driving like a bat out of hell."

"Tell me." Her heart began to pound.

"I was chasing you." He slid his hands up her arms to her shoulders. "I was going to follow you all the way back to Chicago if I had to. I wasn't going to stop until I caught you."

"Why, Quinn?"

He looked around at the field to the east, the dusty road, the black-and-white Holstein cows staring at them from behind a fence on the west side of the pavement. "This isn't exactly the romantic scene I had in mind, but I love you, Maddie. I have for a while." He wiped a tear off her cheek with his finger. "I fell in lust with you the night you walked into the Harp. I turned around and saw you standing at the end of the bar and my heart stopped. Then you opened your mouth and took on J.D., and I started falling in love.

"Please give me a second chance. It's not easy for me to open up, but I swear I'll do my best. And if I back-slide, I'm counting on you to let me know."

"Quinn." She stepped into his arms and cupped his face with both hands.

"I'll keep your heart safe, Maddie." He kissed her gently, a tender brush of his mouth over hers.

"I know you will," she said, wrapping her arms around his neck.

"I won't hurt you, sweetheart. I promise."

She leaned back so she could see his face. "Yes, you will. And I'll hurt you, too. But making up will be a lot of fun."

"Making up? I'm not sure how that works. I've always left before there's anything to make up for." He smoothed his hand over her back, then slipped it beneath her T-shirt. He touched her as if he was memorizing every bump of her spine, every curve of rib, and his fingers lit tiny fires beneath her skin.

His mouth found hers, and she tightened her grip on him. She felt him holding back, trying to go slow, so she nibbled on his lower lip, then soothed it with her tongue. When he groaned, she swept inside.

"Kiss me like you mean it, Quinn," she murmured.

He eased her against the back of her SUV and kissed her again. She pressed closer and felt the tension in his muscles, his struggle for control. She wrapped one leg around his and arched into him.

His kiss turned wild, almost desperate, and she felt herself being pulled under. When she wriggled, trying to get closer, he slid his hands between them and covered her breasts. "Am I getting the hang of this 'making up'?"

"Not quite," she gasped. "But you're almost there. Keep trying."

She shoved his T-shirt up and ran her palms over the hard muscles of his chest. A car zoomed past.

"Maddie," he said against her mouth. "Another minute and I'm going to tear your clothes off. We need to stop."

"You're right." She slid her hands down to his rear end. "We wouldn't want to shock the cows."

He grabbed her arms and brought them to his chest, where he trapped them between their bodies. "I'll follow you back to your house," he said.

A long time later, they lay tangled together in her room, their bodies cooling, her heartbeat slowing. They'd nearly fallen off the tiny twin bed from her childhood a couple of times.

"So I figure you're going to want to live here in David's house," he said, drawing lazy circles on her back as she sprawled against him. "We'll sell my house, and we can use that money to pay the rest of your bills."

Her heart lurched. "Wait a minute. Haven't we skipped a step here?"

"Hmm? What step?" He caressed her bare butt cheek, and desire surged through her again.

"Like talking about the future."

"Isn't that what I was just doing?"

"You were making assumptions, Quinn. You're supposed to ask."

"Ask what? If you'll marry me? Isn't that what we've been discussing?" He slid his hand down her stomach, and she drew in a sharp breath.

"In some circles, it's considered important to actually say the words."

He lifted himself up on one elbow. "All right. Are you going to marry me?"

"I'll think about it."

"Is that right?" His hand slipped lower. "How long will it take?"

"I'm not sure," she panted. "I'll let you know."

Ten minutes later, she was trembling on the brink of another climax. He slowed his rhythm. "Done thinking?" he whispered.

"Quinn!" She tightened her legs around his waist. "Please! Don't stop."

He moved in and out again, excruciatingly slowly. "Tell me."

"Yes," she gasped. "I'll marry you."

He surged into her and she bowed off the bed with a sharp cry. He followed her, groaning her name.

When she could speak, she said, "That was just mean."

She felt him grin. "I've been trying to get the upper hand with you since the first night you walked into the Harp. Looks like I've finally figured it out."

"Two can play this game, you know."

He lifted his head and kissed her. "A guy can hope."

THE NEXT NIGHT SHE WALKED into the Cherry Tree wearing her skirt. As she donned her apron, Quinn backed her against the wall, standing so close she could feel the heat pouring off his body. "You're wearing that skirt again."

"You're really observant," she said with a grin.

"You wearing anything beneath it?"

She raised her eyebrows. "Go out in public without underwear? That would be very naughty. Do I look naughty to you?"

She stepped away from him and picked up a tray. She felt him watching her, and when she glanced over her shoulder, his smile promised that he'd pay her back later.

She couldn't wait.

Laura Taylor spotted her and smiled. As Maddie passed her, the Realtor touched her arm. "I'm so glad you changed your mind," she whispered.

"Me, too." Maddie glanced at Quinn, who was still watching her, and her heart beat faster. It would speed up whenever she saw him, she suspected. Even when they were grandparents.

"Hey, Maddie, I heard you'd quit," Jen said, bumping her hip. "I'm glad the rumor was wrong."

"I'll be working here until I find a newspaper job in the area," Maddie said.

"So you're staying?"

"I am."

Jen whooped and dragged her over to Delaney. Maddie was in the middle of discussing the possibility of Delaney making kitchen cabinets and bathroom vanities for the houses she was trying to sell in Chicago when Quinn slid his arm around her waist.

"You're monopolizing her," he said to Jen and Delaney. "You need to learn to share." He tugged her closer, steering her toward the bar.

"I love you, too, but people are waiting for their beer." She gave him a quick kiss, trying to ease away.

"They won't mind waiting another few minutes." He tightened his hold on her. "Hey, everyone, I have an announcement!" he yelled.

It took a few moments for the voices to settle down. Someone turned off the boom box, and suddenly the restaurant was quiet.

"Thanks, Sam," Quinn said. He grasped her hand. "Maddie and I are getting married."

The crowd started clapping, and Mike Foley yelled, "I thought she was a smart woman."

Over the laughter, Paul called out, "What about running for mayor, Quinn?"

"My future wife and I will discuss it," Quinn said, dropping a kiss on her hair.

He let her go, and pulled a bottle from beneath the counter. It was a bottle of Jameson, about half-full. The glass was burned in one or two places, and soot was smeared on the neck.

"There's a shot of Jameson here for anyone who

wants it," he said. "On the house." He lined up glasses on the bar and poured some of the amber whiskey into each. When that bottle was empty, he tossed it into the trash and opened a new one.

Someone snatched Maddie away, and she was passed from one person to another, each hugging her and telling her how happy they were for her and Quinn. When she finally made her way back to him, he kissed her again.

"You think David would approve of us getting married?" he murmured.

"I think he planned this all along," she said. "I think that's why he broke his promise to you. He was trying to get us together."

Quinn smiled slowly. "David always was devious."

"He told me once that if I gave them a chance, I'd like the people in Otter Tail. He was right." Maddie touched his cheek. "I love you, Quinn."

"I love you, too," he said, kissing her again. He ran his hand down her hip. "Now let's talk about this skirt."

\* \* \* \* \*

*Be sure to look for Margaret Watson's next*
OTTER TAIL *book in June 2010!*

"AREN'T YOU GOING TO SAY 'Fly me' or at least 'Welcome Aboard'?"

Amanda Bauer didn't. The softly muttered word that actually came out of her mouth was a lot less welcoming. And had fewer letters. Four, to be exact.

The man shook his head and tsked. "Not exactly the friendly skies. Haven't caught the spirit yet this morning?"

"Make one more airline-slogan crack and you'll be walking to Chicago," she said.

He nodded once, then pushed his sunglasses onto the top of his tousled hair. The move revealed blue eyes that matched the sky above. And yeah. They were twinkling. Damn it.

"Understood. Just, uh, promise me you'll say 'Coffee, tea or me' at least once, okay? Please?"

Amanda tried to glare, but that twinkle sucked the annoyance right out of her. She could only draw in a slow breath as he climbed into the plane. As she watched her passenger disappear into the small jet, she had to wonder about the trip she was about to take.

Coffee and tea they had, and he was welcome to them.

But her? Well, she'd never even considered making a move on a customer before. Talk about unprofessional.

And yet…

Something inside her suddenly wanted to take a chance, to be a little outrageous.

How long since she had done indecent things—or decent ones, for that matter—with a sexy man? Not since before they'd thrown all their energies into expanding Clear-Blue Air, at the very least. She hadn't had time for a lunch date, much less the kind of lust-fest she'd enjoyed in her younger years. The kind that lasted for entire weekends and involved not leaving a bed except to grab the kind of sensuous food that could be smeared onto—and eaten off—someone else's hot, naked, sweat-tinged body.

She closed her eyes, her hand clenching tight on the railing. Her heart fluttered in her chest and she tried to make herself move. But she couldn't—not climbing up, but not backing away, either. Not physically, and not in her head.

Was she really considering this? God, she hadn't even looked at the stranger's left hand to make sure he was available. She had no idea if he was actually attracted to her or just an irrepressible flirt. Yet something inside was telling her to take a shot with this man.

It was crazy. Something she'd never considered. Yet right now, at this moment, she was definitely considering it. If he was available…could she do it? Seduce a stranger. Have an anonymous fling, like something out of a blue movie on late-night cable?

She didn't know. All she knew was that the flight to

Chicago was a short one so she had to decide quickly. And as she put her foot on the bottom step and began to climb up, Amanda suddenly had to wonder if she was about to embark on the ride of her life.